MY BUDDY

A Commemoration For The First Man Of Jazz

by

Ife-Gail Young

In Honor Of All My Ancestors,
Known And Unknown

Natroy Publishing Co.
NY, NY

Copyright ©2002, 2012 By Gail F. Young

Library of Congress

First Edition
Printed in the United States

MY BUDDY is fiction. Names, characters, places and incidents are historical and/or either the product of the author's imagination and are used fictitiously. Any resemblance to actual events or locales or persons, living or dead, is entirely coincidental.

ISBN: 978-0-9755246-3-3

MY BUDDY

A Commemoration For
The First Man Of Jazz

By Ife-Gail Young

This book is dedicated to the memory of

Charles 'Buddy' Bolden,
The First Man Of Jazz

. . .Also, to my parents, Edward & Mary Franklin, Letitia,
Najee, Troy, Eddie, Preston, Mark (gone too soon), Renee,
Selena, Kinte', to the rest of my family,
relatives and friends; my jazz friends who are jazz
musicians/composers/vocalists; Duke, Rhoda, Shirley, Vern
C., Esq., Vernon J, etc... (You know who you are) jazz
aficionados and scholars who are proud to be entwined
within the legacy of 'King Bolden'

-Special Thanks to Letitia, Najee, Troy, & Vern-

Africans chained in the holds of the boats
Let flow out of their dusky throats
Their culturally rooted musical pizzazz
And enchanted the world with a song called jazz

-Ife Gail F. Young

MY BUDDY

A Commemoration For
Charles 'Buddy' Bolden
The First Man Of Jazz

(FICTION *woven with* TRUTH & HISTORY)

AUTHOR'S NOTES

Written before the deadly hurricane, Katrina, 'My Buddy,' is fiction woven with truth. Fiction: All characters are fictitious. Truth: Buddy Bolden was the first jazz musician in America and jazz has black/ African roots. Also, most historical, social, and political information as well as other tidbits in this book are true. The storyline? Highly possible.

I wrote 'My Buddy,' because Buddy's legacy prompted me to do so. It is just that simple. Furthermore, I believe black people must tell their own stories for the sake of veracity. So, upon being unusually sensitive as I visited my local library one day (This was several years ago.), I discovered an ample amount of material on Buddy Bolden. I developed a bond with him immediately. I was so engrossed, so involved in the greatness and sorrow of the man, that like the characters in this book, Beard and Anwar, Buddy also began to live in my soul. As an artist, I understood that there were several things that posed themselves as adversarial threats to the artistic journey. The following in my opinion, are at the top of the list: certain and/or difficult personal situations and circumstances, unethical contracts and business ventures, and jealous hearted and malicious persons with motives to halt the artist's progress.

Many artists leap over those adversities like hurdles set before one in a race to the finish line. Some artists' progress is hindered as a result, yet, they do reach their goals. Unfortunately, Buddy's artistic progress was not just hindered. It was thwarted permanently. I wept for him.

That same night, I dreamt Buddy visited me. He sat on the corner of my bed with all his essence and his head hung low. When I finally looked into his eyes, I knew I had been appointed a task. Upon awakening, I discovered I'd been left with an undying passion to celebrate America's first jazz musician, a black man, named Buddy Bolden. That passion lasted many years. Finally, I had the time and opportunity to get this book written.

Numerous writers and researchers of various races/ethnicities have expressed a fascination over Buddy Bolden, America's first jazz musician. They have produced factual and fictional books and films but most have glamorized Buddy's life, neglecting to consider the 'Jim Crow' era in which Buddy was born and the racial conglomerates present at that time. Racism reigned and black males were often the target and were hung from trees and Buddy would not have been an exception. However, Buddy did play jazz in New Orleans but only in locations where blacks were permitted, such as in the 'red light district,' and a few other areas within the city. Therefore, Buddy's artistic growth like so many other black performers, was stunted, racism having been the dominant culprit. Few jazz researchers bring that truth to light.

Many facets of Buddy's life in this book, are true. He was born in 1877 (possibly in 1867), was a heavy drinker, sparred with other musicians with his instrument and had made quite a name for himself and his band in 'Storyville' and certain clubs and dance halls in New Orleans.

Before emancipation, enslaved blacks of New Orleans were permitted to assert their cultural dances, rituals and music in places such as on Congo Square. When blacks were emancipated and Jim Crow laws went into effect, an extreme intolerance arose for African-American and African culture of any kind. Furthermore, many black people had been indoctrinated to despise anything cultural coming from Africa, including themselves. As a result of this indoctrination, an enormous number of blacks felt ashamed of who they were and from where they came. So, most blacks felt comfortable asserting their cultural heritage amongst themselves only (i.e, work songs, in church, at festive gatherings). But when Buddy played jazz (black African music) openly and proudly for all to hear, the younger black generations, especially, reclaimed their African heritage quickly. Soon, other races/ethnic groups began to admire and perform black music in spite of the negative connotations placed upon it. It was not long however, that non-black Americans attempted to obliterate the fact that black people created the music they loved and admired so much.

Some researchers report Buddy's music was indeed recorded on wax cylinders but it was also surmised that wax cylinders could not withstand the test of time. Yet, some cylinders had survived. Therefore, can even an assumption be made that Buddy's cylinder(s) did not survive? Perhaps like the character, Gifford, in this book, someone may have Buddy's cylinder(s) stored away amongst other items in their home. That person may not even be aware that he or she has them. Or perhaps the person is aware but might be a lot like the character Giles, thus, not planning to reveal his or her findings. Or perhaps some researcher has already discovered the cylinder(s) and has proudly added them to his or her private collection.

Buddy was committed to an asylum at the age of twenty-nine and that is where he spent the last twenty-five years of his life, laughing hysterically and picking invisible items off the walls. To add even more insult to injury, he has not been given proper acknowledgement for being the first jazz musician in America. Furthermore, far too many musicians have never even heard of him although they play jazz fervently.

Had Buddy not been robed in the defiance and audacity to reclaim and expand on the African rooted music and play it outside of his home, certainly another black musician would have done so because the music was always with black people. But what impact would it have made? However, imagine the void if jazz had only floated out in chants to accompany black men as they worked on railroads or only flowed from the mouth of a brown bonneted woman as she labored in a large cotton field. Imagine the sound having been left in the hold of slave schooners or upon the continent of Africa.

Hopefully, this book will speak volumes to a people who have yet to be acknowledged for their many contributions, from the ancient to the modern world, where for many years this country made it illegal for black people to own patents and copyrights in their names. As for Jazz, it has recently been coined, 'American music.' Yet, history documents it as being called 'Negro music, nigger music, the devil's music, African-jungle, and bushman music, even after the roaring twenties; and as late as the 1930's. The labels were derogatory, however, it is common knowledge that those labels were reserved for black people. How now is it that the origins of jazz are being ignored and is being called 'American Music?' Yes, it is true that throughout the years, like all music, jazz has evolved. White American musicians as well as other ethnic musicians have played it diligently, adding other flavors to it but that does not make jazz something other than Black music. When a song is composed, the composer/arranger and lyricist are forever the creators of that song no matter how many renditions are made of that song. So it is with cultural origins; and jazz.

Meanwhile, black people, continue to fight for every inch of progress, fight for every bit of justice and equality, and in many cases for their very lives and have never been treated as first class citizens. Yet, their inventions are first class? The old saying, 'people want black culture but do not want black people," seems to hold credence. This has been the way for many years, which explains why Dr. Billy Taylor documents the African origins of jazz on the first two pages of his book, 'The Jazz Life of Dr. Billy Taylor.' But let us juxtapose this scenario. Can a martial arts technique that was invented in Asian culture suddenly become American because other races and nationalities began practicing it? Adding to it? Should it be called 'American' because others get involved? No. So it is with jazz. Additionally, not referring to jazz as being 'black, African-American, or African' music is insulting to many black people and is equivalent to leaving the 'European' out as creators of Madam Butterfly and Swan Lake and crediting Asians or Africans as the creators because they perform ballet and opera also. So jazz will always be rooted in black, African/African American music regardless of what others wish to call it.

Additionally, other styles of jazz exist as a result of the transatlantic slave trade. There is Afro-Cuban, Afro-Brazilian, Afro-Caribbean, Afro-Latin, Afro-Haitian, etc.

It is only proper that we give tribute to Buddy Bolden when we listen to Miles, Monk, Parker, Cab, Mingus, Coltrane, Fats, Ella, Byrd, Sarah, Billie, Hancock, Count, Nina, Abbey, Marsalis', Hubbard, Jarreau, McFerrin, Betty, Carmen, Pharaoh, Dee Dee, Joe, Max, Duke, Dinah, Quincy, Nancy, Satchmo, Sonny, Dizzy, Strayhorn, Cassandra, and countless other black jazz artists. They are the 'chil'ren Buddy's horn called home.'

When we visit jazz clubs, we relish in the 'geniustude' that makes us hush and listen. However, few people know the story behind the music, how much Buddy was involved in reuniting us again with our ancestral sound that is so abstract, so profound and distinct, that it lands on the edge of its fond cognizance and swings to its own heartbeat, kisses our ancestral memories and gently serenades our dusky souls. Yes—, I believe jazz does that quite nicely.

Thank you Buddy for the blueprint of our ancestor's song. We are still filling it in; the song that enchanted them, the song that enchants us, the song that enchants the world. The song of. . . scat do be do be bop wa dey___. The song of jazz.

-Ife Gail F. Young

*". . . and it was honestly
conceived. It had been essentially
a memory from where his
weary soul had traveled."*

Chapter 1
Calling His Chil'ren Home

Dedication and musical astuteness had earned Anwar Rasual a M.F.A. in Jazz Studies from a reputable New York university. However, time filtered the use of his degree for he was a musician to the fullest extent of the word. He preferred the bandstand. Yet, education set aside options many musicians had not the privilege of owning. During arduous periods of life, Anwar's 'chump change' was often replaced by 'real money'. 'And just think,' he reminded himself, 'you hadn't desired to go to school at all.' A tremendous respect was bestowed upon his father who had initiated the whole thing. With his foot.

As like most musician desire to do, Anwar yearned to play music all of the time, so work and education were not relevant in his life. Of course not! Would that have not been impractical? School *and* work? So, as his nineteenth birthday celebration extended throughout the weekend and a bottle of Cabernet Sauvignon heightened his musical passions, he entered his bedroom to jam with the jazz masters. After Coltrane's Greatest Hits had blasted out of his stereo at a maximum volume level, an improvisational rendition on electric bass with none other than Monk transpired. They blew the stereo away and the roof as well. But a 1/2" piece of plaster parted farewell to the ceiling and landed in his father's La-Z-Boy chair. In less than a minute, hard soled shoes pounded deliberately upon the stairs that led to the second floor. With a loud *'ugggh,'* the bedroom door was *kicked* wide open and an uninvited figure entered the unkempt universe. He stood watching, unimpressed, as his son displayed his musical proficiency to an invisible audience, stepping over dirty jeans and crushing audio cassette cases, sipping on the crimson elixir. After a few minutes of that display, a calloused hand slid behind the stereo and yanked the power cord from the electrical outlet. Anwar turned to see a tall, sober and solemn figure with an angry and worried forehead.

"Listen here, son," he said in a very unfriendly tone, "I didn't work two jobs all of these years for you to play at this level. If you're going to do it, at least do it right and get something substantial under your belt."

"Oh, not again. I already told you, I'm not interested in going to school," Anwar stated, belligerently.

"You are if you're staying under my roof," his father returned smoothly. "In other words, son, you don't have much choice. But you could get a job and start paying rent like your brother is doing. Back rent would be about, uh, five-thousand dollars and I'll want that up front."

So school it was. But those next six years went by fast. The curriculum that encouraged 'free style' created a juxtaposition that helped him achieve status as one of the *'baddest'* young bassists to emerge in a long time. He had to give an immense amount of credit to Professor Beard for sparking his musical sensitivities.

Beard, a dedicated black jazz pianist and researcher had been his favorite instructor and indeed inspired him to greatness by helping him discover his deep well of passion. For example, he gave a lecture once on the origins of jazz in America and spoke about Charles 'Buddy' Bolden.

"Buddy," Beard explained dramatically, "was the very first to play jazz in the context as it is heard today. He had taken the rags. . . and what do I mean by rags?"

"Ragtime, Sir," answered a young man in the front row.

"Exactly," Beard stated proudly. "And everyone should know who created it and when and where it originated, especially since it will be on your Friday exam. Now, oh yes, Buddy—well, he took the rags and the dirges that most black bands played in New Orleans to another level. Back. Back to Africa. Back to the source that spit it out." Beard smiled brightly as though he were the creator of the music. In fact lecturing his favorite subject, jazz, seemed to be the only thing that did bring a smile to his countenance because away from the classroom, he appeared serious, troubled and stern.

Beard, was a little over sixty. He was a short, muscular, caramel colored man with a square face. His wife was a bit sickly and he sometimes had to end a lecture early if she were seriously ill. He had three grown children and several grandchildren and they all lived out of town so it was just him and his wife. The empty nest they had once looked forward to while raising their children was not what they had expected. It was lonely and futile without the family.

Beard's eyes were small and piercing and he could detect students' lies about homework or a broken alarm clock just by listening to the inflections in their voices. Because of his ability to spot a lie, they usually left notes on his desk and just didn't show up. He would prefer that anyway. He was a stickler for integrity. He was also a sophisticated hip cat if there was such a thing, dressing in dark suits and kidskin leather shoes that shone brightly enough to blind you in one eye, possibly both. And he never bothered to leave the lecture room for lunch or simply browse around campus like most instructors would do. He ate lunch right at his desk and it usually consisted of dry sandwiches, coffee, and for dessert, a stream of jazz books and magazines.

Although he held a Ph.D. in Jazz Studies, students would sometimes forget that Beard had also been a working musician and was hip to the game. He knew every slang word that stumbled into the air too, often explaining to his students that they lacked ingenuity because he used the same slang words they used thirty years ago.

"Jazz," Beard continued with eloquent diction, "is created from the heart. It has no distracting notation as a rule, it just flows. Yes, people do write it out, but one has his way with jazz. It is the music that has reached across the world to demand respect. It is the music that reinvents the soul each time it is performed. Parker knew it. Coltrane knew it. Satchmo knew it. Miles and Dizzy knew it, Ella, Sarah, Monk, Billie, Duke and Mingus knew it and the list goes on. To me, there is no music greater than jazz. Jazz is improvisation." He performed a short scat. "Syncopation and timing." He rapped out a swift rhythm on the blackboard with his knuckles. "And one would have to include intonation!" He hummed a weird melody. The students were so mesmerized by his dramatic exposition that they were unaware of time. In fact, a student would appear highly suspicious if he or she noticed that time had not stood still when Beard lectured.

"Jazz," Beard said, "comes from the soul and forms a language we all understand. And who gave it to us? A young black man that lived on the poor side of New Orleans. A man who played his horn so loudly, that he was heard clear across the river. Charles 'Buddy' Bolden! He once ruined a rival musician's concert. He told his spectators, 'watch me call my chil'ren home,' and he picked up that cornet and blew the hell out of it and sure enough the people made their exodus in groves from the other side of the river to give patronage to their great musical King. His jazz was amazing but racists called it sinful and nigger music. They called it devil's music, jungle music, yet, it was imitated bit by bit and then outright stolen by the same people that had put it down."

Beard stopped short of his lecture, too grief stricken to carry on. Then he shouted angrily, ***"AND THAT GENIUS SPENT THE LAST TWENTY-FIVE YEARS OF HIS LIFE IN A GODDAMN INSANE ASYLUM!*** Oh God, what they did to Buddy!" Then he yelled, "BUDDY!" for an entire five seconds and followed up with a tearful and affectionate, "Oh Buddy!"

Beard's chair became a rest stop and he flopped in it hard enough to damage his spine or even puncture a lung. He held on to the back of it tightly for a moment shielding his face from something ugly and unseen. But he suddenly glared around the room in bewilderment, then lowered his head into his hands and wept a few seconds, quite unaware of his surroundings. Suddenly he looked up and mumbled, "I um—" He could find no words. "Class may be dismissed," he whispered.

The students emptied the room slowly, pity stricken and a bit embarrassed to have seen Beard cry.

"You okay?" a young lady asked. Beard nodded 'yes.'

"Check you out, man," another student added.

"I feel it too, bro," one young man said, knocking on his chest.

Awkwardly tall and extremely skinny, Anwar, stopped at Beard's desk. He was visibly shaken. The most prominent thing about him at that time was his crop of thick, wooly, hair. He crouched and whispered in Beard's ear. Beard lifted his head quickly. He was astonished. A student had actually felt his sentiments? He appeared pleased to observe the tears that flowed down Anwar's cheeks.

"Professor Beard, please—please say that great man didn't fade away just like that," Anwar pleaded.

"Just like that, he did. I'm sorry son."

Beard sniffed and blinked away a tear. Then a sudden flow of tears splattered on the polished oak floor, each one a defiant miniature puddle. Anwar's tears followed, mixing with Beard's and from that day on, he and Beard formed a unique relationship over the love and loss of Buddy. For years to come, Anwar would play his bass with Buddy in mind. He would develop an undying passion to honor the man that would become an integral part of his world.

So Anwar Rasual had been playing his upright bass throughout the mid-northern and eastern regions of America with some of the most prolific musicians in the country. But after several years of semi-successful recording, sitting on overstuffed suitcases, unwanted hassles of the music industry, including late or smaller than expected royalties; downing greasy fast foods; change had been sought. A putrid weariness of the road and the weightless life surrounding it necessitated roots, for he had begun to go in the direction of the thousands that had gone before him: *'the infamous lifestyle of the traveling musician.'* There were the late night hours, too many cigarettes and cocktails, loose relationships, recreational use of drugs, and a bit of irresponsibility. But amazingly, his body remained strong and taut. His spryness was offset with a non-categorical, unconscious, philosophy of life. A little deep, a little selfish, a little uncertain.

The reflection in the mirror revealed Anwar as an elegant creature. He was naturally trim and muscular with wide, square shoulders. Those attributes combined with a height of 6'3", once won him the title of 'Mr. Sophistication' in a jazz periodical. And there he stood reveling in his appearance as he buttoned the jacket of one of his many tailor made suits. Arrogant, so many had called him, for his head was held extremely high on all occasions. He'd inherited his mother's good looks, people said, minus the facial hair, of course; a goatee and moustache, which were cleverly connected while his tapered sideburns added character. A chocolaty, smooth complexion set off his sensual, 'full' lips and the arch of his heavy eyebrows made him appear strong and mysterious and the women often ran a fingertip across them in a flirting game. Top all that off with a close haircut, lined meticulously from front to back and it is no wonder a woman walked up to him and said, "Mister, I have to tell you—you are just too fine.'

For several years, unlike Beard, the latest styles in fashion had been his folly but the conservative suit staring back at him in the mirror would be quasi-essential for the time being. It would be dry cleaned, then assist him in passing inspection from the scrutinizing eyes of interviewers who often ostracized applicants that dressed too trendy. There could be no loyalty to such things as fashion when his cupboards were empty. Bottom line, he needed a job!

Chapter 2
Opportunity Personified

A full professorship practically landed in Anwar's lap a few weeks after submitting his resignation as band leader. "Don't go," they had begged but the road had beaten him down. So he'd sent out resumes and the first interview was with Jacob Giles, Head of the Music Department in a relatively unpopular and new university in Connecticut that had a predominantly white student and faculty body.

'Everybody's white,' he said to himself as he peeped inside the small classrooms. 'Now what the hell is this all about?' he wondered. Foremost on his mind was who had they assigned to teach jazz?

A thin white student worker sat at the reception desk. She was heavily freckled and wore three golden loops on one side of her nose. Blonde and lime green dreadlocks drooped lazily down her back and were 'topped' with a striped conductor's cap while faded tattoos ran up and down her arms. She licked a fingertip and wiped away the shine above the black drawn on brows that gave her a tragic appeal. Then preparing to speak, she moistened with her tongue the mouth that was caked with black lipstick. She smiled at Anwar first then said, *"be very careful—"* But she stopped when Jacob Giles, a short, pudgy, blonde and gray, balding man rushed to the area. He gave the girl a distrustful look as he extended his hand almost violently to Anwar. The girl turned toward her computer. Fearfully.

8

"Jacobs Giles here. And you are Anwar Rasual?"

"That I am," Anwar said, shaking Giles' hand.

"Well, come into my office," Giles beckoned to Anwar but weirdly enough he whispered, "that young lady is one of our most gifted students but unfortunately, she hasn't carried her musical excellence into her appearance. She looks awful, doesn't she?"

'Why make the appearance of a student a subject qualified to comment upon,' Anwar thought. 'Sure, the girl did have a frightening edge about herself due to the makeup but a lot of young people dressed like that. It was a fad.' If Giles thought the student would make him not desire a position at that university then he thought wrong. But that statement made him wonder about Giles. Why would a person in an administrative position be concerned about such triviality? The student was practically a kid. Of course, he didn't say that to Giles but gossip was reserved for people with small minds and goals and that definitely was not his calling.

They entered a plush office and Anwar's eyes were immediately drawn to the large picture window that overlooked the busy highway.

"Beautiful, isn't it? That window keeps me sane in this place. I spend seventy-five percent of my time staring out of it but don't tell anyone. Have a seat, Mr. Rasual. And you can relax. I don't give a damn about that asinine protocol they call interviewing. You're not on display here."

Innumerable plaques and awards were affixed to a gray stone wall. Anwar gazed at them for a few seconds, quite impressed.

"Are these your—

"Yep. Those are all my doing," Giles answered before his interviewee could finish the question. "You see, I used to play diligently. Piano. I got married though and didn't that shit put an end to everything good. So, listen, I don't care what goals you have five years from now, what kind of work you've done in the past or whether you've been fired or have gotten into trouble with the law, none of that is important to me. All that matters, is that you can play the hell out of an instrument and that you have a M.A. in Music and I got the perfect job for you—on one year, off one year. How does an Associate Professorship grab you? Now I'm not talking Assistant."

"Associate? But I'll need a track record as a professor and a Ph.D. for that, won't I?"

"Maybe not. You have a lot of experience as a musician, don't you? Now let me explain. I'm a jazz lover and an avid researcher. Matter of fact, that's mostly what our department has focused on for the past ten years, research. Now, please don't get embarrassed but I especially need a black professor on my team for three reasons. First of all, it will satisfy the demands of our contract; that we maintain a certain percentage of minority faculty members at all times. We only have two now. And secondly, you would most likely be the best candidate because you are rooted in jazz and last but not least, you'll also be the best candidate for going amongst your people and bringing back factual information.

"Going amongst my people? I don't understand."

"Well, going around the blacks of New Orleans. But once again, let me explain."

Giles lifted a small paperweight and fumbled around with it as he collected his thoughts.

"Alright, here it is. I've sent several white researchers amongst the blacks of New Orleans for information and they were chased out every time. Some even returned with broken bones and blackened eyes. So, it only stands to reason, that the people want one of their own kind creeping around them. And apparently that old attitude of 'shucking and jiving the white man' still exists. Black people are still reluctant to give true facts to whites."

"Well, they could be a little inhibited, I suppose," Anwar chuckled. "After all history does give us reason."

"Oh, that's so ridiculous. What happened to your people was in the past. And it was my forefather's doings, not mines'. To think, they still do not trust white men! Why that's absurd! Bottom line. Kerplunk!"

"Well, I beg to differ on that, sir. My people are still suffering and I think the forefathers have been dead for about uh—what?—three hundred and fifty years? So somebody these days are still making sure things don't change for us." At that point Anwar didn't care if he did or didn't get the job. How dare Giles insinuate that black people only suffered in the past!

Giles was caught off guard for a minute. He appeared jittery but did not respond to what Anwar had said. He took a deep breath, composed himself and continued. "I even sent the last two professors with six expensive guitars and two keyboards to present in exchange for information. They accepted the instruments, but I'll be damned if we could get the people to talk."

He thought about that for a minute. "Hmmm, well, maybe they didn't give the instruments to the people. I'll have to remember to do some research there. Now, what would you like to do? Just lecture or teach performance?"

"You speak as though I have no choice in the matter. Isn't this about me? My life too? What about the contract? I'll have to accept it first."

"Oh, that goes without saying. Associate Professorship? I know you will accept that. All I need is for you to say that you're ready to make money and ready to be a team player for this university. How's your knowledge of jazz? You are still into jazz research, aren't you?"

"Of course I am."

Again, Anwar had Beard to thank. When in college, he'd assigned Anwar course work at the Schomburg Center for Research in Black Culture, an archive located in the heart of Harlem. He'd gone through thousands of photographs and snippets and was simply mesmerized over jazz and the lives of musicians. Ask him anything at all about jazz and he'd know it right away. Anything. Yet, this could not be a spur of the moment decision. It would require deep thought and consideration.

"The research is not the problem, Mr. Giles. I still conduct research. But I can't commit to a job right away."

"Well how long does it take to decide something like this?" Giles inquired, quite restlessly.

"If I will accept a job like that? At least a few days or so."

"I wasn't speaking of accepting the job. Any thinking man wouldn't hesitate. It's a once in a lifetime opportunity and this job can set you up for the rest of your life. So I already know you're going to accept the job."

"Then you know more than I do."

"I believe you are correct to assume that," Giles said with a crooked smile. "Listen, I really want to know if it will be lecture or performance you'll teach so I can update the school bulletin. You can do both too, you know." Giles was not prepared to take 'no' for an answer.

"Well I can't say just yet. There are things to consider."

"It will be to your advantage, of course. Again, all I need to know is what you'd like to teach. It's all on you."

"Well, let me, . . . just let me think about it. Every job I've ever had that seemed too good to be true usually was."

"Hogwash! People that won't take chances think like that. You didn't strike me as being traditional or a follower. I didn't get that impression at all. But— are you?

"Traditional? I've never had herd mentality if that's what you mean. I think for myself," Anwar returned, nearly defensively.

"You know," Giles continued, "my father always told me you have to be in it to win it."

Giles voice faded as Anwar wondered why a university's faculty staff in year 2000 included just two people of color?

"I saw the recording studio on my way up. State of the art. Is it reserved for students only?" Anwar asked eagerly.

"It's all yours."

"Does the department offer financial backing for original recordings?"

"We will for yours," Giles answered with a smile that made Anwar very suspicious.

"Now, the curriculum…is it designed by the department or would I be able to design my own?"

"Do whatever you wish."

"How many classes would I be required to teach?"

"Your call."

Giles rose and began laughing softly. He paced the floor; a beautiful black quarry tile sealed in thick grout.

"Mr. Rasual, it's obvious that you are trying to find flaws in this proposition. Can't you possibly believe that you just happened to be in the right place at the right time?"

"But the job is not clearly defined."

"Is any job ever clearly defined in the beginning?"

Anwar thought deeply about that. Giles might have been on point. He'd known employees to write the job descriptions as they filled the positions.

Giles sat upon the corner of his desk with his arms folded. He looked self-assured in his finely made suit. Anwar sized him up. He knew about clothes and Giles was wearing the best. No doubt he was pulling in six figures, maybe a hundred and fifty grand. And he had confessed what his work had consisted of mostly. It wasn't counseling students or performing administrative tasks. It was *looking out of the window.* What a life!

Silence floated around the room a few times. What would he do? Take the job? He studied Giles, who had begun to pat his foot impatiently. Giles knew why Anwar was so reluctant and finally blurted, "you can call your own salary. Tell you what, bring me a list of your requests and we'll sit down next week to discuss them. How about that?"

This was too strange to Anwar. Questions of all kinds presented themselves in his head. But he imagined having an office with a picture window as large as Giles' and spending most of his time gazing out of it as well so he put aside the questions. But this was a puzzling proposition indeed. He would have to discuss it with Merriam. She had demonstrated time and again that she possessed an uncanny insight unsurpassed by anyone he'd known.

"Oh, Mr. Rasual," Giles continued, "be prepared to start this fall."

"But Mr. Giles, I'm concerned, as a matter of fact, suspicious when a position such as this one is awarded to me without merit. After all, an instructor is a vital component in the life of a student and may be a determining factor in that student's future achievements. How do you even know that I'm qualified?"

"I just know. Relax Rasual. You'll do fine. Being perfectly honest, if I may, and please understand that this is not a discredit to you in any manner, but—

"Yes?"

"Well as I said, it's contractual reasons first of all. We must bring aboard a black professor but we must do it within the next few weeks or we are facing a huge lawsuit. Ummph—you can't imagine how embarrassed I feel right now telling you this."

"Oh, now I understand."

Anwar sat back down wondering what else Giles would reveal. Certainly there was more to come.

"Furthermore, . . . that New Orleans assignment?" Giles continued, "well, I'm the one who needs the information. You see, I've written a lot of material on jazz but this next book is going to be my signature piece, so to speak, the one that will be my legacy to students in the form of a textbook. I know that I should have said that before but I would have appeared self-serving. I was hoping I wouldn't have had to say anything at all about it. Not today."

"Well, looks like the cat's out of the bag now, I guess. It would have been easier for the both of us if you had just told me. If I take the job, I said *if*, then I would expect a truth centered relationship with my employers. So, now I know. I will be assisting you in writing your next textbook. You've written jazz documents before so you've accumulated quite a bit of research I assume?"

"Precisely. See up there? That's all my jazz research."

Giles reached upon a shelf and removed a thick notebook that was full of photos and interesting articles on jazz. Anwar browsed through it quickly and was very impressed, especially because there was extended information on Buddy.

"Now next sabbatical would be all yours," Giles continued. "But we must get that textbook written and published, son. It's crucial. I want to see it stocked high on shelves at every campus bookstore on earth. It will teach the world the truth about jazz."

"The truth? Hmmm. I thought the truth was pretty well documented," Anwar said, glancing at Giles with a sound of distrust in his voice.

"But there are other perspectives. Of course, they won't shake what we already know but there's always something to add to the stew to give it a different flavor. You know what I mean? You're a researcher. You understand what I'm getting at." Giles gave Anwar that crooked little smile again then grabbed his notebook.

A loose handshake from Giles almost convinced Anwar to walk away from the proposition while he was in one piece. He'd been taught a firm handshake meant sincerity and trust. A loose handshake meant the opposite. Still he rose to leave, feeling a bit special to have even been considered for such a coveted position. With a slight smile he thought about the 'token Negro' and how he must have come about. Ideally, no one could be more token than this job would make him. He'd be hired based solely upon the color of his skin. Certainly though, as Giles had implied, he would have the privilege of writing his own contract. That, he would make more explicit in benefits than imaginable to the graft oriented fat man. And yet, New Orleans would be worth the classroom confinement and the time and effort required as well. He'd finally get the chance to search for relics belonging to Buddy and perhaps dedicate to the genius' memory an entire chapter in Giles' future textbook. But what if Giles were cynical, he thought? Well then he'd have to outsmart him. But how? Maybe he'd request a sabbatical first, just in case Giles would decide to fire him as quickly as he wanted to hire him. Yes, that's the kind of proposition he would bring to the negotiation table, not omitting a request for an automobile with all expenses absorbed by the University, within reason, of course. Indubitably, the pendulum was swinging in Anwar's favor. It wouldn't be Negro tokenism after all. It would be opportunity personified!

"Anwar, good day. I mean that," Giles said sincerely. "I know you'll make the right decision."

'Anwar? He called me Anwar'?

A chuckle followed as he left the office. Giles was already on first name basis. As he passed the student receptionist who was bent over the water fountain, he heard, "pssst." She quickly pulled him to the side and tucked a note into his hand.

"Keep this to yourself. Please!" she begged.

The girl seemed terrified. Anwar thought she looked like something out of a horror movie with her black lips and eyebrows in a panic stricken state. But he was courteous and assured her he wouldn't say anything. He read the note just before stepping inside the elevator. It read simply, *'Watch Giles.'*

What was this? What had she really intended to say? He hated mysteries and this was the worse kind. Now she had gone and complicated his decision. *"Watch Giles for what, dammit?"* He would have to ponder that note and the position for the entire weekend.

When he reached his house, a cute little wooden two bedroom ranch, cheaply made, he could see Merriam's image floating back and forth past his kitchen window apparently 'laying out' a meal. He threw the car in park and let his seat back. *'Watch Giles,'* he repeated. Would he let that one little note repudiate the entire proposition? He'd never been able to stay in New Orleans as long as he had liked because his band maintained such a busy schedule. Each time they had played there, they saw little more than the clubs or hotels they were booked in and eventually their tours were limited to the northern states. So maybe he would 'watch Giles' once he was on staff. 'Never mind the warnings that came from students that disfigured themselves with holes and tattoos and dyed their hair green.' She might have been the ultimate expression of 'weird. 'Hell, she had probably concocted all those suspicions of Giles in her 'new wave' brain. She might have been suspicious of anyone that dressed in a suit and tie, including me,' he thought. He laughed aloud to think of her green streaked dreadlocks and wondered what the African Masai would think of them.

Chapter 3
A Woman's Intuition

The air was warm and thick with a fishy stench, yet, unlike the polluted winds in the befouled section of the city that kept him in full-blown sinus infections, this air was amazingly clean and medicinal. Anwar took a deep whiff of it and gazed upon the horizon that was always so pompous and magnificent before the dusting of an orange sunset. He was awestruck as he gazed upon the peaceful surroundings. He watched a father pulling a child in an old fashioned red wagon, an old man with bad knees making his way up a hill with the help of a tree branch, a woman with an array of honey yellow to fuchsia colored wildflowers tucked into the band of a floppy sunhat, a squirrel trusting enough to enter a gazebo occupied by screaming children and beg for food. These simple things he'd grown to respect. But his favorite sight was the silhouette in his window. He loved when Merriam was cooking in his kitchen. 'She needs her own restaurant,' he'd said many times. Her domestic qualities brought balance to his bachelorhood. With her, he had all the benefits of marriage without tacky commitments. Admittedly, marriage was something he'd never planned on becoming acquainted with although he was thirty-six, childless, and growing no younger.

Ah, Sweet Home. He had purchased the tiny house in cash and moved in the very next day. His mother begged him to find a sturdier place but he was happy with it. His house had been built about eighty years earlier when an influx of fishermen appeared with nets and small boats. The waters would provide their income and give them the opportunity to 'grow into' Connecticut. Yet, their new homes, in all their essences, had been built in a place reserved for 'old money.' Any property and land worth possessing had already been taken. The banks and hotels had been built, the libraries and museums already stood proudly, businesses operated fluently, and the roads had been tarred and flattened. But the small group of poor fishermen still built one story framed homes, breaking almost every architectural rule conceivable. The results were crooked windows and doorways, interrupted electrical services, poor insulation and wooden floors that were wilted and unstable from dampness. Some houses sat front to front, others back to back and some sat adjacent. Anwar's and Merriam's houses sat back to back. Both were built with several aged, wooden beams and appeared as though they would disintegrate should a defiant and restless wind head their way. But Anwar was well satisfied with his home for he had wanted to be anywhere that a club was not, where a busy street was not, where lots of people were not and especially where he could lose himself with Bassetta, his upright bass. Merriam wanted to get away too. She had once lived near a seaport when she was a child and loved nothing better than to look upon miles and miles of water and sky.

Merriam walked into Anwar's life the first week he'd moved there. He was reluctant to enter a relationship with a woman that lived so closely. He'd have no privacy! So he made his home uninvited to her for months by shutting off his porch light whenever he saw her heading his way to borrow something or to just talk. She was beautiful, no doubt and he found her hard to resist but he was sooooo tired of women interfering with his career. But he changed that tune after a few dramatic episodes with ladies he'd met at clubs. One had broken out two of his windows in a jealous rage and another had keyed his car when he called it 'quits.' He soon learned how to appreciate a levelheaded woman like Merriam. Besides she was intelligent and a wonderful conversationalist, like himself. They began dating and never stopped; spending extended time in one another's homes so often until the houses became essentially the same, both his and hers.

The scent of a meal assaulted the air. He deciphered it as chicken and gravy and his mouth watered profusely. He let the car seat back further as he pulled his long legs from under the dashboard of his small sports car, his second very old vehicle. "Go Merriam," he whispered. She was an excellent cook and would put pretty veggie garnishments on his plate, usually parsley and carrot cutouts.

The mailbox needed screws replaced like yesterday. He'd meant to get around to fixing it but preparing and sending off resumes took precedence. He reached into the old iron box and held it firmly to keep it from gliding as he caught hold of the mail in his large hands. There they were, the notorious, threatening bills, sent by companies eager to cash in on his home that he'd listed as collateral for a loan when he was still traveling and performing. Lately, it had seemed as though the mailbox was reserved for bills only. The residuals from his recordings had not been at all hefty and he was a little behind in practically everything.

Merriam greeted him with a long wet kiss. Her tiny nephew was there and had been whining but stared curiously as Anwar's and Merriam's lips met. As soon as the kiss was over the little boy screamed, "Anwa, Anwa."

Anwar leaned over and gave the child a little kiss on the forehead then reached into his pocket for a peppermint.

"Uh uh," Merriam cautioned. "Give that to Auntie. No din din, no candy." Merriam grabbed the treat.

"I don't like vegeeebul," the little boy pouted.

"You wanna be strong like me, don't you, and go at it all night long?" Anwar joked, smiling at Merriam. She shook her head at him, disapproving of him speaking that way. Of course the child hadn't understood but he yelled out, "NO!" He then pouted and folded his arms.

"Alright then, you're gonna get sand kicked in your face at the beach," Anwar said. He and Merriam chuckled while the child somehow sensed they were laughing at him.

"Oh, doo doo," the little boy shouted.

"Jua, no no. Bad word!" Merriam warned the child to watch his mouth then turned to Anwar dangling a wooden salad spoon.

"What?" Anwar asked.

"How'd it go? That's what."

"Oh. Well—I think I have a job."

"What? Already?"

"Yeah. If I take it."

He began by telling her about the college, about Giles, New Orleans and the job proposition. He didn't tell her about the student's note though. He expected her to be excited but the more he went into detail, the more she drew her face into a frown. Finally, she could hold her tongue no longer.

"Anwar, That man has a hidden agenda!"

"And so do I. New Orleans. Buddy Bolden. Fame and riches. I can finally go there and look for his stuff. He had to leave something! Hey, maybe I can stumble upon that cylinder. Me and Buddy would be famous world wide."

With an exasperating sigh, Merriam replied, "people have looked for Buddy's things for years? And I don't know what kind of college head is going to come right out and say he needs a black man to go to New Orleans."

"One that is honest, apparently. But I guess you couldn't fathom him being honest that way either."

"No, I guess I couldn't. I told you I would help you with your bills until you found a job. A decent job."

"I don't want my woman taking care of me. If anything, let me take care of her."

"You sexist. Just don't you let that man send you to New Orleans to do his dirty work."

"Dirty work? Merriam, the man would go himself but what would it look like for a white man to be wandering around in an all black neighborhood in New Orleans?"

"Gathering information? Strange and suspicious. So, he will just send you in his place. And you're so eager that you can't even read between the lines. And Buddy's stuff belongs to our people, not you! But Anwar wants to get fame and fortune from them. Hooray, go Anwar!" Merriam threw her fist up in the air.

"Merriam, just stop it."

"Stop it, nothing! You're gonna take the first job offer because you can go to New Orleans for free?"

"A whole year for free! Now who do you know can do that? With all expenses paid?"

Alright, then do it. I'm not getting into it this time. Every time I warn you about something I turn out to be right anyway, don't I? Well, let's just wait and see what happens this time."

"What do you want from me, Merriam? Okay, alright, I won't go. I'm gonna let you clip my wings, baby. Ya happy?"

"I don't clip wings. Do what you want. And don't lean back in the chair, you're gonna break it."

Merriam had begun to sound like his mother. As much as he loved her she could make him feel slighted, little boyish-like without ever having tried. He could imagine himself sitting with her fourth graders with his hands neatly folded on top of his desk. That made him lean further back in the chair. Defiantly.

"Alright, you're gonna break it," she said again.

"And so what," he retorted childishly, "it's mine!"

"That it is. It's definitely not a style I would allow in my house," she said with a sniggle, then turned to remove a pan from the oven. "Perfect," she mumbled. Nearly every dish was though. Never did she make the mistake of adding too much salt or pepper or giving anyone indigestion.

"You know you're exuding sexuality bending over like that," Anwar said, flirting heavily.

"That's not what I'm trying to do so get it out of your mind, please."

"Have we ever made love on the kitchen table?"

"Anwar! Watch your mouth. You know he repeats things."

The little boy looked at them both as though he understood. While he had their attention he made his requests known and began to cry, "no eat, no? No eat?"

"Anwar take him out of the chair, please."

"Anything for you, baby. Pretty thang."

Merriam seldom paid Anwar any mind when he was insolent like that. She shook her head while he lifted away the tray to the high chair and stood her tiny nephew upon his feet. Little Jua quickly made his get away to the other room, leaving his vegetables untouched.

Anwar continued watching Merriam, admiring her large rounded behind and small waistline. If you didn't know Merriam and met her when she was sitting down, you would think she was a bit on the thin side but when she would stand up you'd see differently. She was what Anwar's mother referred to as 'bottom heavy' and warned him that Merriam should be handled carefully. Old folks would refer to her as a 'heavy breeder'. The size of a woman's hips and breasts were a dead give away as to how many children she'd be capable of 'spurting' out. Merriam was a few years younger than Anwar but appeared to be in her twenties. She was about 5'8" and weighed a hundred and forty pounds. Her skin was butter brown smooth and her face was full and framed with a head full of natural, kinky hair that she wore in braids and twists and adorned with scarves, beads and cowry shells. She didn't wear makeup but she had used astringents and moisturizers for years, so her face was a luminous statement in itself. She also ate right and all those healthy practices teamed up with one another to give her a look some women would spend thousands of dollars to get. Was she attractive? You bet she was!

Chapter 4
Classrooms Or Stepping Stones?

Anwar thought about Giles' proposition long and hard over the weekend and decided that he would definitely take the job and he wrote out his requests carefully and selfishly. To his surprise Giles consented to everything he had listed except he would have to teach at least two semesters before sabbatical. He was already being awarded an Associate Professorship without having all the required credentials but nobody had ever been granted sabbatical without having taught a class. But he tossed that out there anyway feeling he might as well take advantage of everything he could. That type offer would never come again and hell, they needed him.

"I'm damn important around here, Anwar, but I don't have that kind of pull," Giles stated, flatly. "Just no can do. Now, yes, my best friend is Provost of this University and whatever I want, I get. See, we were boys together and fraternity brothers but for the sake of saving all three asses—

"Three asses?"

"Damn right! Mine's, his, and yours! Let's just play it by the rules til summer break. Just give me that much time in the classroom. Huh? Would you?"

Anwar obliged. After all, teaching jazz studies would be a cinch and summer break would be upon him before he could say, Charles 'Buddy' Bolden.

That fall found Anwar wearing strong reading glasses and tossing chalk from hand to hand in the large lecture rooms. He had decided to teach two music appreciation classes and coordinate the jazz performance series. The first week consisted of many questions and answers.

"Who in here plays jazz?" he had asked the roomful of yawning and stretching music students. Practically all of them raised their hands.

"Ah hah! Now does anyone know who the first musician in America was to play jazz?" The students talked softly amongst themselves, speaking names and dates aloud. He thought it very amusing that some white students said jazz was developed by Bix Beiderbecke and the three or four black students said it was sang and the syncopated beat played on pots and pans during slavery.

"Alright," I'm going to answer the question. "First of all, Bix," Anwar said melodramatically, "came along much later than most early jazz musicians, about 1923. Buddy Bolden had played jazz in New Orleans from about 1899 to 1907. Buddy Bolden was a black man and he was the first American jazz musician because jazz has African roots. It was a style that was familiar to most black people. Buddy did something a little special with it and that style came to be known as jazz."

The whispering and talking that had rudely taken place while he was speaking suddenly stopped. One student, a white young lady, raised her hand.

"Got a question?" Anwar asked, expecting many of them.

"I do," said the young lady dressed in pink from head to toe. "Professor Giles said the Original Dixie Jass Band more than likely started jazz and they were white. Who are we supposed to believe?"

"I think you might have misunderstood Professor Giles," Anwar said thinking of Giles book of research. "I'm certain he said the Original Dixie Jass Band was the first white band to record jazz *after* Buddy. There's a difference."

"No, he did say that," added a young man in dark shades. Other students spoke up as well. They all claimed Giles had taught them the first jazz musicians were white.

'If Giles had believed that himself, he wouldn't be sending me to New Orleans', Anwar thought.

"Well, it's simply not true," Anwar said a bit defensively. "Professor Giles is a very knowledgeable man and I doubt if he'd ever tell any of his students that intentionally but we professors tend to get things confused ourselves from time to time. But the best thing to do is conduct some research on your own."

Most of the white students were taken aback, while the few black students sat erect in their chairs with their chins tilted up. Their pride was as obvious as whistling in the dark. Then one white student stood and said, "this class is bullshit." He walked out and a ruckus evolved.

"Okay, settle down everyone. Walking out is no big deal. Quiet. Now it's been said that Buddy made the first jazz recording before 1906. None have been recovered but the search goes on. Alright, read the next two chapters and be prepared to discuss them. Class dismissed."

That week the students told him a few other things Giles had taught them contrary to what had been documented in jazz history. Anwar just summed it up as Giles having a very confusing teaching style.

Surprisingly, Anwar had a natural talent for teaching but it clashed tremendously with his playing. Sometimes he exited right behind the last student. He'd lock the door and dash to the lobby where several coffee vending machines were located. He would drink a few cups then rush back to the room to await the next class, far more alert than he was before. That would be an easy day. Those days when the coffee didn't work were long and grievous.

Toward the middle of each semester, punctuality became a problem. Sometimes his students would sit waiting for fifteen minutes or so. He would rush through the doors with his laces untied and his shirt cuffs unbuttoned, bumping into desks and lecterns, appearing confused and nervous. Those were the 'morning afters', when he'd gotten in the house at 4:00 a.m., determined to salvage his musicianship at a club. Those mornings Merriam would call his house five or six times and he still wouldn't answer. She'd rush over with a pot of coffee and a breakfast sandwich. If he had slept at her house she would place an ice tray on his back or forehead. He would wake up roaring, swinging his arms and kicking and fussing.

One morning she warned him, "Anwar, you're gonna have to let the music go for awhile. You know what they're gonna say if you keep going in late, don't you? CPT."

"If they want to say I'm on 'colored people's time', let them. Let em get the watermelon and chit'lings out while they're at it too. Oh hell, Merriam, I don't care what they think. I have to play Bassetta sometimes. I have to. I shouldn't have chosen those morning classes. I'm a 9-5 puppet, baby. I'm the white man's puppet. He tells me to jump and I have to say 'how high?' Really. And I can't stand it!" He intentionally knocked over a cute vase Merriam had bought him to add a little color to his dull house.

"If teaching is going to affect you like this, then just quit and join your band again and struggle to pay bills and don't complain about empty pockets," she said, humoring him.

He might have quit if he wasn't making over seventy-thousand dollars for an eight month assignment and if New Orleans wasn't the carrot that was leading his cart. There was nothing that would turn him around. 'Teaching would bend his branches a bit but it wouldn't make them snap,' he thought. If all the other teachers could hold on, so could he. Furthermore, it felt good to catch up on his bills.

Ironically, he and Merriam had grown closer. She often sat across from him grading tests or planning activities for her class. He finally understood why she griped over the demanding workload of teachers. He, a freelance musician at the time, once insensitively barked back, "oh, come on now Merriam, stop complaining. Teaching can't be that damn demanding." How wrong he'd been. He found out that teaching could be a hell of a job.

Sometimes he would cross over to Bassetta and play her for about ten minutes then go back to grading papers, fussing and cussing. He complained once, "all this work for the damn system. I got a pile of essays to read where my young people just rattle on and on about nothing and never make their points. God! It must be the hormones. I dread reading those papers. I'm just gonna give them all a damn 'A' and be done with it." He smiled, relieved he had found the solution.

"You can't do that. What about the students that really deserve an A?" Merriam contested.

"As long as they get their 'A' they shouldn't complain. Besides I don't want to miss George Benson. I missed him last time."

"He'll be here again, Anwar. Just do what you have to do."

"I have to do me. I'm a musician."

By the end of the second semester his nerves had been worked thin enough to keep his stomach in knots, he'd increased his cigarettes to more than thirty a day and he jerked nervously at the sound of sirens and noises at construction sites. But in spite of the tedious undertakings his position had required of him, he had somehow found time to pack his suitcases and tuck them underneath his bed for that magic moment.

The second day of summer break was ordained as Anwar's 'harvest of the classes day' and his crop was bountiful. He received a voucher to lease an automobile for a whole year, got a university credit card, a place to stay and plenty of spending cash.

Giles peered at Anwar suspiciously and said, "I don't want a half assed job. You gather as much information as you can, especially photos and memorabilia of the marching bands. Get news clippings, old instruments, anything that can document that early sound. And interview! A lot of people! Don't bring me back three or four interviews. I want to know what the social life of a marching band member was like and who wrote out the music. I'm sure the people there had grandfathers that marched and could tell you something. And don't forget to do research on early white marching bands too. And I'm not keen on verbose and hyperbole. That's a dead give away that the research is not up to par. Less is more. Keep it simple."

Giles had asked nothing in comparison to the amount of research Anwar had to conduct on the obscure Buddy. Would people in New Orleans remember anymore that Buddy had been the first to play jazz? Who would care? Buddy had been almost a household name in New Orleans at one time but the years gone by had dipped menacingly into the gaps between generations and had lifted away meaningful cultural and historical data. But Anwar couldn't speculate. He'd been surprised by how many people did know something about Buddy.

Once he told a musician friend, "hey man, Buddy Bolden was the first jazz musician, not King Oliver."

His friend gave him a puzzled look and squalled, "man, I thought you was educated. Jazz was the sound that came out of the hold of the ships. It came with us from Africa, dude. Didn't that fancy college teach you shit? Bolden just expanded on our African sound."

He'd often wondered about that. To hear the sounds of syncopated chants, harmonized and rising like black smoke from the hold of a slave schooner would be too much for him to handle. He would die of emotion. Beard too. In fact Beard had already suffered a heart attack due to emotionalism. It caused him to retire from teaching and Anwar often found him at libraries bent over jazz books, taking a few moments each hour to educate the busy librarians on none other than jazz.

Anwar had been under the tutelage of Beard since his college days but their relationship had changed throughout the years. No longer was Beard just teacher and mentor and Anwar just student but they were like best friends, maybe like father and son. They valued one another's company and Anwar respectfully assigned Beard the position of Elder and treated him accordingly. They confided in one another, advised one another on important matters and supported each other in times of need like when Beard was in a dilemma about having a triple bypass. Beard's children were there and gave their opinions but he valued Anwar's most.

The impulse to drive over and check Beard out before leaving was overwhelming but Beard would understand if he couldn't make it. He would call him after he had arrived. Furthermore, he hadn't wanted to tell Beard the truth, that he was going to New Orleans to gather information for a white jazz researcher. Beard would be so disappointed in him. He would say, 'you are letting a white man send you to New Orleans to pull information from our people for *his jazz textbook?* Are you out of your mind?' Beard distrusted practically all white jazz researchers because he'd often undergone verbal combat with them and white jazz enthusiasts. Beard surmised that most white jazz aficionados wanted to claim jazz as their own people's invention.

'Nah, best to see Beard when I return,' He thought. Beard had always felt that Anwar was his best student and to let him know the initial reason for his going to New Orleans might taint his image. And Merriam? She hadn't even known that he was leaving. He wanted to put off telling her until the very last moment because she would surely make a scene. He decided to visit one of his favorite clubs and jam with a few of his buddies. He would deal with Merriam the next day.

Thank goodness, the door didn't squeak as he turned the doorknob at 2:00 a.m. Hopefully, Merriam was at her own house. He kicked the table as he tipped into the dark room. "Ah, shit!" Stubbed his toe! He hopped and yelped.

"That you, Babe?"

"Damn!" Merriam had been sleeping on the sofa.

"Come here, Boo. Mama missed you. Where you been?"

She rose and kissed him hard. She had other things on her mind but he couldn't get into the mood until he'd told her about his leaving. He had to do it right then, while he could muster up the courage.

"Merriam, something happened today."

"Huh? Something like what, Babe?" Anwar paused. She appeared afraid. Her eyes widened. "Like what, sweetie? Something bad?"

"Well, it depends. I saw Giles earlier. I'll have to leave for New Orleans tomorrow."

"What?!" Merriam sprung off the sofa.

"I just couldn't get out of that damn sabbatical!"

"Oh Yeah? And I bet you tried real hard!"

"Okay now, Merriam! You fulfill all your job obligations, don't you? Don't you?"

"You knew you were going all the time, Anwar. I'm not a fool. Admit it. What are these?" She reached under the sofa pillow and pulled out travel guides. "New Orleans!

Every last one of them! Why would you have them if you weren't planning on going? You're full of shit, Anwar!"

"Well, serves you right. You had no business looking under my pillows anyway. Awww Merriam—

"Don't . . . don't you touch me. Just leave me alone. You're a snake waiting until the last minute."

"I'll only be gone a year."

"Only! A lot can happen in a year . . . and how could you accept sabbatical without considering me? I could have found work in New Orleans if you had told me and we could still be together." She began to cry. "I would never do that to you!"

The last thing he wanted was for Merriam to follow him to New Orleans and take up all of his research time but of course, he couldn't tell her that. He tried to put himself in her shoes and the thing that stood out most was that she really didn't understand his passion.

"Merriam, listen, listen, baby. I've wanted to go to New Orleans since my freshman year in college." Merriam didn't want to hear excuses for him being a snake.

"You didn't need some unheard of university to pay your way. You spent enough money to have gone ten times by now. But no, you wait until you get into a relationship!"

She snatched a tissue from the dispenser then inspected it as though it were distrustful too.

"Listen Merriam, if it makes you feel any better, you can join me this summer when I get settled in."

"And do what? Follow up behind you while you ignore me like you always do when you're researching something?"

"That's a lie! When have I ever ignored you?"

"When you coordinated that 'Tribute to the Saxes' program. That's when they used you to get that grant. Oh, you remember. They got a little black brother with a degree behind his name and they nearly worked the hell out of you, didn't they? And did those saxophonists respect a bassist telling them what to play? Hell no! Now look at you. This time you're being shipped off to New Orleans like a good little Negro boy that has no life, no future, no woman but maybe you don't. Hell! What do I know?"

"Oh please! What was I supposed to tell Giles when he asked me? No, I don't want to go because I think you're just using me? Merriam, everybody is not out to get the black man."

"Well, that man is. It's so obvious to me. And yes, you should have told him, 'you're using me.' And he *is* using you. You're supposed to keep our culture, not give it away. That's how we lose our credits as a people. But no, we have to let the white man in on everything! You said yourself that jazz was like a secret society sound and we could share it but have to protect it from culture vultures. And you just told me a few weeks ago that you thought everybody was trying to steal the black man's credit for inventing jazz, remember? Well, now you're helping them cause you're falling right into the trap!"

"Not by a long shot because it appears, my fine black woman that I'm going to be doing the using this time. Wait until you see how much of Buddy I bring back."

"Yeah right, Anwar. Just leave me alone. And by the way, I have been holding something inside for awhile now. You've changed since that job put a little money in your pockets. It's made you arrogant and you have no regard for people like you used to, not even me. I've watched you. The old Anwar would never have waited until the last minute to tell me he was going away for a year. You had a much better personality when you were still in your band."

Merriam gathered some of her belongings then let a stream of cold water run for a few seconds before filling up her glass. She had lost so much in the past few years; the baby, and now she felt as though Anwar was joining the list. She sipped from the glass, looking toward the ceiling as if she were entranced by an image in the kitchen. Anwar felt sorry for her. He wanted her to know that he did love her but this was an opportunity of a lifetime. "How am I arrogant now?" he asked. She didn't respond. But did she really feel he hadn't considered her as much as he fretted over telling her he was leaving? He would fix things.

"I wish you wouldn't keep drinking that tap water. I told you the water around here is no good." There. That would prove to her that he cared.

"Then get a filter. And like you'd give a damn anyway!" she returned. "Besides I cooked all your foods with it, which means you're full of lead too. And that's not all you're full of. I'm going home."

"Home? But I thought you were sleeping over here. And since I'm going to be lea—

"Sleep over here for what?" She suddenly felt an edge over him. "So you can try to get a whole year's worth of sex from me in one night? And after you deceived me? Hell no! I doubt if we'll ever come together again. You never even gave me one hint that you intended to go. Not one." Powerfully, she repeated, "I'm going home. Home, Anwar."

She slammed his screen door. The corner of the wobbly wooden frame broke off and fell across his feet. "I'm going to charge you for breaking my door," he shouted playfully. But she was in no playing mood. She held up her middle finger and kept walking.

Chapter 5
Where Buddy Was

The next morning Anwar jotted down some details that needed to remain fresh in his mind like where he would go in reference to where Buddy had been born, lived, worked, played and died. He wanted to visit Buddy's gravesite and see if he could get some kind of spiritual connection. But then again, he had read that other coffins had been piled on top of Buddy's. If flooding would take place, the weighed down coffins were less likely to float away. He read on and discovered alarming news. He quickly dialed a number. The professional male voice at the other end said . . .

"New Orleans Jazzin' Up, Inc., how can' I help you?"

"Yes," Anwar said, in a very dignified tone, "I will be in New Orleans to conduct research and would like to know if there is any validity in what has been written, uh, that Buddy Bolden's coffin may no longer be where it was buried? I read where it may have shifted to another spot."

"Sir, I would be unable to support that statement."

"Why can't you? Are you saying that I would have to come to New Orleans first to find out if his coffin floated away to God knows where? I need to know this."

"Sir, I do believe it would still be in that cemetery. Our soil gets very moist at times so it would be to your advantage to investigate that for yourself. I could be held accountable if I were to give you information that is misleading."

"Well, can you tell me the kinds of songs his family passed down? What kinds of secrets had been revealed about Buddy? I mean, you live in New Orleans. Buddy's a legend. Can you give me any information on him at all?"

"We are not an agency that provides answers to those kinds of questions over the phone. I recommend you pay us a visit when you arrive and we will be happy to accommodate your requests."

"Well, tell me this. What do you know about Buddy Bolden?"

"Me personally?"

"Yes, you."

The voice said, "I will be more than delighted to discuss Buddy Bolden with you in person. What we know about him is included in our archives. You're more than welcome to browse through them. Because we are a reference library, you will not be able to take the materials with you, however, you will be permitted to make copies of—

"Yeah, yeah," Anwar said quite distastefully and hung up.

'Buddy's coffin gone maybe?' Unbelievable. Where the hell would his coffin be? Had it shifted or had it floated away?'

That was the most distressing and depressing news he'd heard in years. He was extremely shaken up about that and wanted to tell Beard but thought it best not to. Instead, he left out to pick up a few extra things needed for his trip but he did tell a few others about the coffin expecting to get strong reactions but that didn't happen. Instead, some people said, 'oh yeah? Who's Buddy Bolden?'

He visited Merriam and tried to kiss her but she turned her head. They sat staring at one another for nearly an hour, neither speaking a word. Perhaps they were bonding in a strange sort of way. Finally Anwar gave in and spoke.

"Merriam, you're acting just like you're twelve years old. This is a temporary assignment, that's all. You have to understand I'm doing this for us both," he stressed.

"It's not benefiting me. It's benefiting you. And you have no tact. That was mental abuse you put on me; springing New Orleans up at the last minute."

"However, I said it, you would have been unhappy about me going. Can we just hold each other before I go?"

"Hold your damn train tickets. That's what you should do," she said, as malevolently as possible.

"Come here you," Anwar lifted her out of the chair and carried her to the living room and tossed her on the sofa. When he pressed his body on top of hers', she bit him on his shoulder. Really hard! She left a mark.

"Don't you dare play with me as though what I feel doesn't matter! Why don't you just go? GO!"

He'd never seen her that angry. He had wanted to give it to her 'good' in case she had it in her mind to do a little venturing. Merriam was too attractive and too much of a good thing to leave amongst those flirtatious wolves in the area without putting a 'hard to top' loving on her mind. He thought it best to give up on the idea though after she had wobbled her head and rolled her eyes at him for ten minutes. Reluctantly, he scribbled out a little note and taped it to her refrigerator. It told her when he would arrive and where he would be staying. He kept his eyes on her until he was out of the door. She didn't call him back—so she was left sitting solemnly at the table with her mouth poked out.

The next visit would be with his parents. His father would over praise him while his mother of course, would wish him well but conjure up some supernatural warning and that would probably haunt him for several days if not weeks. Later that day his brother, his only sibling, dropped him off at the train station in Manhattan.

"Ey man, you take care of yourself, now. Don't let me hear about somebody whipping your behind."

"Oh, get outta here," Anwar said, shaking his head. "You make a lousy big brother, you know that?"

"You know trouble got a way of finding you. You think I don't know that, huh Bro?"

"Yeah, yeah. Alright. Can't you just wish me well?"

"You know I do. Gimme a hug, man."

Anwar gave his brother a tight hug and a few pats on the shoulder and disappeared into the terminal.

He'd decided to take the train because it was the form of transportation that could best help him relax. He never relaxed when he was in the air. He'd scold himself for allowing an invention of man's to take him so high where he had none or little chance of surviving should something happen. But he enjoyed watching landscape flash by while riding trains. It always created for him a mood of detachment. After riding an hour or so, he was completely relaxed. But he was worried about Merriam and felt like a dog for not letting her know he was leaving. It would be safe to call her after about a week to apologize again. Hopefully, she would be okay. He opened his book but reading was difficult because a small group of people talked far too much. He'd never liked associating with people who talked too much and strangers always did. They'd talk about spouses, children, jobs, finances. If someone tried talking to him he planned to put in his earphones but if the earphones act didn't work, he'd bury his head in his book.

The train pulled into New Orleans a day and a half later and it was hot and humid. Cabs were lined up in front of the terminal and Anwar quickly claimed one. The cab driver was annoying though. He looked international, like he could have been born in any country and Anwar could not figure out his ethnicity even when he spoke. That wasn't important but the fact that the man ran his mouth so much was. Who could relax? And they hadn't even left the terminal. If it was a tip the man was looking for, well, he blew it. Maybe he could have put up with the driver's mouth if he had spoken about something relevant but it was as if he was stuck on stupid, disturbing his vibe, gabbing away about nothing.

They finally reached the shipping unit where Bassetta sat and Anwar somehow got her into the back seat of the cab.

"I can't see out the back window. Would you move that thing?" the driver complained.

"Move it where? And it's not a thing, it's an upright bass," Anwar defended.

"I know what it is but I got to drive this thing."

"Well drive," Anwar insisted.

"You know how much they charge me for insurance? You know how much I have to pay if I have an accident?"

After shifting Bassetta this way and that, her bottom rested partially in the space behind the front seat and partially on the back seat and stretched across Anwar's lap. Her neck, protected by the hard plastic case, protruded out of the window. The driver still complained and warned that he would not be responsible should anything happen.

"So what ya' want me to do, leave it?" Anwar said with a threatening stare.

"Maybe you can rent a small van or something."

"No, I need it tonight! Man, just drive the cab!"

Anwar was not about to have his beautiful illusion of New Orleans smeared by a finicky cab driver.

As they made their way through the city, the driver showcased his ignorance by calling cellos 'guitars' and trumpets 'saxophones.' Anwar gazed dreamingly out the window wishing the man would shut the hell up and allow him to feel the pulse of the city. He wanted to communicate with the ancestral spirits and also see if he could identify landmarks that had appeared in the tourist guides but the man chattered on. When he pulled up too closely and hit the curb, the instrument case shifted and struck the metal molding strip on the window. The driver put on a wry grin as Anwar gave him a dirty look. He got out and paid the driver just fare and commenced to unload his own luggage. A young man happened to be passing by, nibbling on fries.

"Hey bro, need help?" he asked cheerfully.

"Yes, I do. You mind?" Anwar replied, grateful he had offered.

"No, not at all," the young man assured. He tucked the nearly empty food bag into his jeans pocket and began helping. He had so much stamina that he practically carried all the luggage himself. Anwar thanked him and tipped him nicely.

"You know what you gave me, sir?" the young man asked, surprised and quite modestly.

"I know what I gave you. I want you to have it. I really appreciate you showing up when you did."

"Well, I would have helped anyway. But this is a. . . lot."

"So now you have enough to take your girl to the movies, right?"

"Take my girl? I can take my whole family. Thank you."

The young man put the six ten dollar bills in his wallet and walked away with a noble gait.

The apartment was part of a huge complex. His place was nice but it had only three rooms: a large living room with gray carpet and a black leather sofa and ottoman, a bedroom with a queen sized bed and an older styled dresser and a kitchen that was adjoined to the living room. It was relatively modern. It had a dishwasher and an ice making refrigerator/freezer. The bathroom was modern also but very small. There was barely enough room between the toilet and wall to relieve oneself comfortably. Anwar's long legs would be in for a big surprise. There was also a working phone in the living room. Overall, the apartment was a cozy little space and that's all he had needed for what he had gone to do.

While glancing through the window, he spotted a small village-like arrangement of specialty boutiques. Pedestrians hurried across the streets, visiting and leaving the shops. His eyes lit up, "whoa, I've get in those streets!" So he unpacked quickly, showered, then jumped into a lightweight pair of slacks and a printed shirt that gave hint that he was a tourist. Afterwards, he browsed through the listings of jazz clubs in the French Quarters placing a small pencil mark by the ones he would visit. He slipped on dark shades that made his tourism status even more apparent and by 5:30 he'd left to pick up his rental. He chose a brand new silver-gray Chevy SUV, big enough for Bassetta and headed promptly to a popular jazz location, thinking of Storyville and what it had meant to early jazz musicians.

Storyville held as much fascination as a ghost as it had when it thrived and neighbored the French Quarters. It was the world renowned 'speakeasy' section of the city that had somehow emerged on its own accord. It had sent its infallible red light so far that it hypnotized some of the most prominent politicians and notable figures, calling them to sample its wares of scandalous affairs to great blues and jazz singers, to large hipped prostitutes and jumping juke joints. He'd read so much about the jazz clubs and how any good musician could earn a pretty decent living working there, that he often imagined himself on the stage with Buddy and his band and playing with Jelly Roll, and Joe 'King' Oliver, speaking to them in a distinctly cool manner.

"Ey, looky here Jelly Roll, tinkle those keys on the high end and Joe's gonna accentuate your sound with a sweet, 'melojous' tune that's gonna make the ladies weep and howl. Buddy's gonna take lead and stand everybody up in their chairs and I'm gonna

drop a riveting bass-line on 'em, ya dig? A one, a two, a one, two, three, four—

Zoot suits and colorful fedoras had been fetishes of Anwar's as far back as he could remember. He imagined mean pimps in zoots and highfalutin madams fattening their pockets and purses from brothels that entertained the poorest to the wealthiest of men, white men. He'd learned it had been illegal for black men to have sex with the prostitutes in Storyville, including black prostitutes. Racism was present in all social spectrums.

Buddy had been right there, playing for everyone, the wealthy, the poor, the decadent. That was the one place he had felt accepted and the place where people gave him credence for being the first and the baddest jazz stylist in the City. They loved Buddy and spread the word about him. But Storyville was just the beginning. When Buddy would sought evolvement on a wider scale, discordance would be sure to challenge his dreams.

Bourbon Street was a crowded, noisy area, boasting old structures of early French influence, smoldered in vivid oranges and forest and olive greens and yellows that seemed to come alive with the music that bubbled out loudly from nearly every club and cafe. People sat eating New Orleans famous beignets and drinking hot chocolate while others formed a long line to taste New Orleans style gumbo. Most of the people there were more than likely tourists. Several were visibly intoxicated from drinking huge amounts of alcohol and those who weren't intoxicated were busy snapping pictures of those who were. Practically everyone was uninhibited. Some of the younger men went shirtless and appeared wild and animated. They roared and beat their chests and tussled with one another in front of clubs and pretty women, each vying for the ladies attention. A lot of the women were scantily dressed, barely covering their bosoms and some skirts were little more than twelve inches in length. Then there were the women that limped and carried their high heels while onlookers shook their heads pitifully at the sight of their red and tender bunions. Of course there were the debonair men that said things like, "forget the shoes, sweetheart, I'll carry you."

Thousands of romances had began in that mystifying, hypnotizing and lewd piece of land. Men even flirted boldly with women that walked arm in arm with their significant others and vice versa. About six young women wearing form fitting slacks and dresses danced to the music of an old standard that flowed out of a club, *'when we're out together dancing cheek to cheek.'* They swayed their hips side to side and flirted with the single men that passed them by. One said, "look what I found," and grabbed Anwar's hand. "Dance," she shouted. He resisted but finally broke into a dance with them. When he started sweating he escaped and stood watching. He hadn't seen those many attractive women partying together since he'd stopped playing the clubs regularly. Nice eye candy for his first day.

Theatrical or Halloween costumes were worn at all times in the French Quarters and nobody found it strange. A man and woman were dressed like vampires with such authenticity that Anwar wondered why they were out in the broad daylight. 'Vampires couldn't go out in the daytime, could they?'

'Hey,' he said, catching himself. 'What's wrong with me thinking like that anyway? Those kinds of thoughts will make me doubt my own sanity', he mumbled, scolding himself for that type foolishness.

Souvenirs and artwork were for sale at the galleries and small retail outlets. Proprietors sat eating cheese and bagels sold by vendors on the stretch. A woman robed in a burgundy and black gypsy costume sat at a table with Tarot Cards, flipping people's hands over and tracing their lifelines. She beckoned for Anwar to come with a bent finger and three inch nails. He declined.

Shiny beads, and feathery masks were worn by at least one third of the people and beer flowed high and formed an arch as it was squirted off terraces by young people from oversized toy space guns. They huddled together and laughed wildly as it left stains on the clothing of tourists. Some people enjoyed it and opened their mouths to catch the beer and whatever else was tossed or sprayed. A beer storm greeted Anwar as he made his way under a terrace. He had no choice but to join the jubilee and expect those things to happen to him as long as he was in New Orleans. Hopefully his shirt would be dry by the time he'd enter the clubs. Somebody gave him a string of Mardi Gras beads and shouted, "don't take them off, man, they're good luck."

"I won't," he shouted back. Luck was surely what he was going to need when it came to researching the eminent, Buddy Bolden.

An awesome band was performing at one of the clubs and he was tempted to head back to his apartment and get Bassetta but he had had a hard enough time finding his way there less lone heading back to do it all over again. Besides, he wanted to feel the mood of different spots before 'hitting' at them. A beautiful caramel colored woman dressed in pink and green ostrich feathers and a sequined pink and green gown swayed her hips with her legs spread wide singing Bessie Smith songs, shouting *"Judge your honor, hear my plea, 'fore you open up yo' court. I don't wan' no sympathy cause I jes' cut my good man's throat... send me to the 'lectric chair."*

"Wow, this is interesting,' Anwar thought and stood against the back wall to hear more. A great applause followed her act. Then the trombone player stepped forward and blew with all his might. The patrons went into a frenzy, screaming and dancing. Those were songs Anwar was not familiar with but his parents would know them and Beard too.

"Play it! Play that!" he shouted along with others.

A few people almost dived on the dance floor to get a spot before it was overcrowded. The singer and the trombonist broke into a dance routine that excited the crowd so much that people rushed towards them and tried to grab their hands or pull feathers for souvenirs as if the band was world renown. "Move away! Give them air," shouted a huge security guard. He stretched his arms out wide and pushed the people back.

The woman sang *"I know a fool really blows a horn. He came from way down south. I ain't heard such blowing since I was born, like when dat trombone hits his mouth – Well he wails and moans. He grunts and groans. He moans just like a cow. Nobody else can't do his stuff cause he won't teach dem how. Oh Cholly, play that thang, play that slide trombone. Make it talk, make it sing...*

People laughed and made room for the animated horn player who danced around while playing the old jazz tune.

"OW!" somebody shouted near the middle of the crowd. "You're stepping on my foot!" That was Anwar's cue to move on. He knew the signs of a fight.

He entered a huge club with a beautiful black and white checkerboard floor. The jazz there was a lot different than that of the east coast. Obviously, some of the music was for the sake of tourists who expected New Orleans nostalgia to drift amongst the scenery. It included old Rags, Underground Blues, Dirges and even Zydecos played with vintage accordions and washboards. There was also the distinct sound of steel pans. The entertaining steel pan drummers permeated the eclectic musical atmosphere, moving their arms and hopping so rapidly until they seemed to be only a blur. Bands cheered one another on and took turns going onstage. A crowd began to gather and Anwar made his way over to see what was taking place.

There was a black dwarf couple dancing. Neither was taller than three and a half feet. No doubt they were professional dancers and they found no problem drawing the people who applauded and cheered them on. The man dipped and flipped his partner and she slid and swung on his arms with ease. Five, ten and twenty dollar bills were thrown at their feet. But apparently a routine act went sour. The little man spun his partner around then lifted her and tossed her wildly at the crowd. She hit the floor head first.

The people shouted, "OOH, WHOA," in unison. The little woman was dazed. She shook her head and lifted her body slowly. The little man ran over to help her

"Move. Jest move outta my way. Where's Tone? Where the hell is he? You knew he wasn't there to catch me. You did that on purpose to make me quit! Get outta my way."

"I wouldn't do that. I didn't know," the little man yelled.

The little woman refused to believe the man had not plotted a conspiracy to end her career. She elbowed her way through the crowd and refused to let anyone help her. She had a knot on her forehead the size of an egg and 'people being people', began laughing at the couple and imitated the woman being thrown to the floor.

As the couple continued to argue downstage, a jazz band assembled upstage. They began playing almost immediately after the tiny couple had gathered the scattered bills and left.

The band's horns resembled miniature suns dancing over mounds of brown earth as the musicians swung their bodies in unison and played harmoniously. Their cheeks bulged with air. The patrons swung along with them, clapping and stomping their feet and shaking their heads. The musicians sweat profusely. It dripped into their eyes and soaked into their tux lapels, seersucker and polished cotton suits and onto their ruffled shirt collars. They were feelin' it. They stole sips of water skillfully between beats, and still kept the groove. The music resembled swing with a huge big band flavor. People danced to it the way they danced to rhythm and blues, their hips shifting from side to side, their pelvis' gyrating, old school hand dancing, fancy James Brown footwork, and the New Orleans shuffle. Others did their own thing. They spun across the floor and performed slick moves that were applauded by onlookers.

"Over here, babe," Anwar called to the cocktail waitress. "Gin and tonic."

The pretty cocktail waitress swayed with the music and made him a drink. He moved closer to the band. A few more drinks followed and he found himself pining because Merriam had not wished him well. But then the band began to hit so hard that he could not help but get into the groove. He patted his foot and made wild gestures as if he were playing his 'ax.' When the set ended he made his way to the stage and introduced himself to the musicians. They seemed very willing to tell him where the hopping clubs were on the black side of town and which ones he could hit at and get paid. He thanked them, gave out his business cards, collected a few business cards himself and called it a night. But before he left he asked a few of the musicians what they knew about Buddy Bolden.

"What we know about him?" a musician repeated loudly with a drawl. "Man we are him. This Naw__'Lins! Where you from?"

"Connecticut."

"Connecticut? Aw shoot, Connecticut don't count fo' nothin'," the musician slurred. He and a few others laughed wildly. The man had spoken so disrespectfully. It was as if Anwar wasn't even there at all.

"So what's funny about east coast jazz? Coltrane and Miles tore up the east coast. Even Yardbird developed his style on the east coast," Anwar rebutted.

"Yeah, yeah," a big, heavy set musician puffed. "That's what all yawl clowns from the east coast try to whip on us. But the real live shit happened right here, my brotha. This is the place where jazz comes from the *soul*."

"What? Are you saying we don't have soul on the east coast?" Anwar asked defensively.

"I ain't saying nothin'. You just said it for me."

"Oh, come on now, brother." You're separating the music. We got the same African roots. We're all the same black folks."

"Uh uh. We ain't nothing like the east coast. We can play!" Again, the men laughed, especially the heavy set one.

'So you scored with a bunch of laughs and confirmations. So what!' Anwar mumbled. 'Laugh all you want, fatso,' he said to himself. 'You won't laugh for long.'

He concurred quickly that those musicians did not know what the hell they were talking about. He might as well just leave. "Well, play yo' asses off then," he said to those still laughing, then he crossed in front of the fat smart mouthed man to shake the keyboardist's hand. At least he was a cool brother and knew his history. He assured Anwar that east coast jazz was 'happening'. But Anwar had tight jaws. He wanted to punch the smart mouthed musician. He thought, 'who the hell was he to discredit a black musician when they had all shared basically the same culture? Their ancestors had come from some of the same places in Africa, had experienced the same oppression. A rambunctious brother like that, he thought, had to be convinced by Bassetta. What's the use in arguing?' Yet, as ready as he was to let it go, the overweight musician was not. He backed into Anwar on purpose and caused him to fall to the floor. Then he ground his heel into Anwar's shirttail.

"Oops, sorry," the man said and burst into laughter.

'Oh! So this was how it was going to be'? Anwar thought. 'Aw hell naw!' And the fight was on! He rose and punched the musician. The musician grabbed a microphone stand and using it like a bat, swung at Anwar. It made a whirring sound and Anwar felt a quick breeze sail across his face. A few of the man's buddies were able to duck and dodge, missing getting tagged by the stand's iron disk. They were finally able to pry the man's fingers back and remove the makeshift weapon. Then they dragged the furious and intoxicated musician into the men's room to try and calm him down. Anwar hung around until the men came out of the bathroom. He hadn't wanted them to get the impression that he was afraid of them. But he hadn't come all the way to New Orleans to be involved in arguments and fisticuffs. That was childish. Now he appeared thuggish. But he would've never earned respect from other musicians if he had not fought back. He finally left the club, slowly, shaking hands and nodding his head until he was out of the door. But he would be back the following week with his credentials. He would bring Bassetta to the bandstand along with a few of his CD's and give Naw__'Lins a sample of the eastern kin.

As he drove home he thought about the complexity and diversity of African culture and felt a rush sail quickly down his spine. Blacks were everywhere, he thought. All were ultimately different, yet, magnificently the same.

Chapter 6
King Bolden Time!

In spite of the immeasurable amount of research; Anwar and Bassetta had managed to win musical respect in less than a month's time. Some musicians revered Anwar's style and skill so much that they would not play with other bass players, nor would they start programs until he had shown up. Club owners would gloat over his presence, rushing to the stage as though they were announcing the arrival of royalty.

"And ladies and gentleman, the most prolific bass player in the area has just entered this establishment, Anwar Rasual. Let's give him a warm round of applause. And you'll want to fill your glasses now because you are not going to want to be interrupted when he takes the stage."

People would stretch their necks and twist their bodies to get a look at the virtuoso bass player and if they were planning to check out another club, they kept their seats until after Anwar had played. They also spent more money on drinks so the club owners got the best of two worlds for an hour or so.

But Anwar had worked hard, almost nonstop to collect enough material and documentation to satisfy Giles too. Yes, he had experienced some difficulties in obtaining the facts. Museums would not let him take pictures and he could not check out certain books and documents from archives. Then there were the people. Some just would not talk, fearing the facts would be modified as so many researchers had done. But he pressed on. Besides what Giles had wanted was almost 'in your face stuff'. He would collect a bit more information before his sabbatical had ended but it was finally time for the prize research. Buddy!

Anwar discovered some researchers claimed women and being overworked drove Buddy mad; others said the alcohol did it. Buddy's last performance was in a Labor Day parade. Anwar's eyes started tearing. He needed a break.

"Man, this city is hot. Are we next to the equator or something?" he asked a plum colored man standing next to him at the newsstand wearing a sweat drenched hat. For some reason he didn't take Anwar's question lightly.

"You don't like the heat, get out of the fire," was the middle-aged man's response. He slapped a dollar on the counter, folded his paper and placed it under his arm and began sifting through salty snacks.

"You know who Buddy Bolden is?" he asked the man.

"Don't insult my intelligence. Do I know who Buddy Bolden is?" The man repeated the question but he never did give Anwar an answer. He walked away and looked back to give him a scowl every few seconds.

A young woman, the color of a brown paper bag had apparently listened to the whole conversation and gave Anwar a smile and a bit of advice.

"You're new here, aren't you?"

"Yeah, you can say that," he answered, puzzled.

"Well, my advice to you is not to say anything bad about this place. I came here to go to school and I have learned to shut my mouth if there's something I don't like about New Orleans. The community in California was the same way when I was in undergrad. I think people just take things personal when you insult the place they call home."

"But I never insulted him. I just asked him a question. A simple question," Anwar clarified. "It wasn't personal or offensive."

"Well, undoubtedly, he doesn't like those kinds of questions. I'm just saying. I had to learn the hard way."

"Oh yeah?"

"It's a long story but if you can't say something good about this city, don't say anything at all. It's just better that way. Hey, have a good day."

The young lady walked away quickly without even paying for her goods. She looked tattered as if she were having a hard time. Anwar could relate. He barely had a dollar to spend when he was in college too."

He studied the different newspapers, chose one then moved toward the cooler. After a few minutes, he crossed over to the counter to pay for his items.

"That will be—uh, eighteen dollars."

"What? I only have a newspaper and a bottle of water."

"You pay too for girl, right?" the Chinese man asked.

"No, I don't know anything about paying for her stuff."

"She tell me, you pay. She lie? I call police on her."

"No . . . wait, wait, wait."

'Ah hah! The young lady had entered into a conversation with me to make the attendant think we knew one another. She hustled me and the attendant. Wow, she was slick.' He marveled over how easily she did it too. She was so skillful and so honest looking, convincing. But she was also a snake. And she was probably not even a student but one thing was for certain, by the appearance of her clothing and sneakers, she was having a hard time. He didn't want her to go to jail for something so trivial. He'd spent eighteen dollars for just one drink when he went out on the town.

Disgruntled, he paid for the young lady's goods and headed to his car. He was embarrassed that he was such a pushover. He should have been able to recognize a hustler. He could in Connecticut. He thought about a song by Stevie Wonder, *"Living For The City."* If he wanted to survive a tourist attracted place where hustlers ruled and prey was plentiful, he'd better wise up.

The red light crept up on him while his mind was on the incident. He rode through it carelessly. A traffic ticket would be his lesson upon a lesson for trusting everyone. He wouldn't talk to strangers again. No, he would but only for the sake of research but even then he would have to be very careful. He looked in his rear view mirror as he drove away. Good. No police on his trail.

A few blocks from the newsstand, a young lady laughed and put away her rejected food stamps. She tucked her brilliantly acquired goods into her book bag then made her way to the next newsstand thinking 'she was elaborately up on her game' or her suckers were just getting dumber.

New Orleans seemed to grow hotter with each passing day and the people became more colorful, almost like the blooming of flowers: pastels, blues, oranges, and reds. Crickets were jazzing up their songs and the mosquitoes were presenting themselves a nuisance on his windshield. But that was Naw__'Lins. Besides the mosquitoes 'buzz' was syncopated.

"This is it, this is it," he mumbled to himself as he checked his map. He made his way to see Preservation Hall, where Buddy had performed. Anwar sang softly, *"I thought I heard Buddy Bolden say, you're nasty, you're dirty, take it away---I thought I heard Buddy Bolden shout, Open up the window and let the bad air out, open up the window and let the bad air out."*

Many buildings were gone but he wanted to go into their vicinities. There was Tin Type Hall, Globe Hall and Odd Fellows Hall. And he knew Buddy had been in those areas because he experienced a strange sensation, like when Bassetta was talking nasty sixteenths to him in a jam session. Then he imagined Buddy, Pops Foster, Robichaux, Keppard, Jelly Roll, King Oliver and a few others, all ghosts, standing outside and playing what they knew best, with Buddy playing loudest. He snapped pictures of one area then returned to his car and drove a short distance, headed for the location where Buddy had supposedly spent fifty percent of his time drinking and kicking it with his friends.

He reneged on going to Buddy's grave but after visiting his house he started questioning passerbys about him. Younger people shrugged their shoulders, unconcerned. A handful of neighboring older people watched him suspiciously, angrily. Had this been xenophobia? Buddy had been their legend that was denied by an unapologetic south. One woman whispered to her husband, 'here stands this skinny black man wearing a suit and tie on a hot ass day, looking as Negroish as possible and writing things down about Buddy. Look how he snubs his nose at us."

"What the hell he want?" the husband asked. "He best to leave our Buddy alone! Hadn't he been stomped on enough? I think we outta put a stop to him snooping around like this. He just outta watch it if he knows what's good for him." Their stares chilled Anwar to the core.

But it didn't take long for him to get his routine down to a science. Morning hours were reserved for research while evening hours meant he would hit the clubs. But . . . that didn't last long. Playing finally took precedence and he started living in the clubs. He noticed that a lot of black clubs had been patronized so completely by white tourists. He often asked them, "where did you say you were from?"

"I'm from Holland—

"I'm from Sweden—

"I'm from Germany—

"Me? From Russia and you?"

"I'm the one that started jazz," he would reply with a grin.

Most of them would say, "oh," not understanding the connotation, of course. But the tourists were always 'in the house'. They packed the more popular black jazz clubs so tightly that he seldom got a seat or could barely squeeze by them. He didn't think Buddy would have approved of him not being able to rest his feet. But the jam sessions were awesome. Addictive. White musicians were also on the stages and tourists pulled out their instruments and joined the jam sessions. "I got to get more work done,' he'd thought. 'Gotta get back to Buddy. Stop sleeping so late' Time was flying by but he hit the clubs hard. Couldn't stop.

Nobody had ever been able to convince him that anyone could feel the pulse of jazz as much as black musicians or people of color. He had played with a lot of other cats and could not feel the same cultural connection and energy that he felt with the 'brothas and sistahs'. It was as if most black musicians knew who they were and where they had come from and that knowledge sealed a bond between them. It was also as though the music was the one thing they had that could not be taken away. So few things in American society had intended to include those who came in chains and their descendants. A lot of black musicians had in common, doors being slammed in their faces and little things of substance being available to them that could propel their lives forward. So perhaps something planted deep inside their stories automatically attached itself to a 'like' consciousness and bonded with the souls of people like themselves. What poured out of their instruments, then, might really have been an ancestral DNA memory, a secret society sound, a connection, a sacred content riding with the adornment of skill. Who knows? But black musicians had always felt an ownership of jazz. Perhaps that heightened

their passions even more. The results were an empower-
ment and intense sensitivity that just led them 'out there'.
Sincerity. He felt sincerity in all art forms was a necessity.

On the other hand, he believed a lot of white musicians
had taken their schooling too seriously and were overly
concerned with counting and keeping the original melody
rather than taking the tune to another level. That put a block
on his connecting with them. A lot of black musicians and
musicians of color had never had formal music education
and relied on their feelings to lead them 'out there' and they
connected differently with him. But he had to admit that
he'd played with white musicians that did touch that space
in 'jazz,' and connected with him, Sinkburn had; a middle-
aged trumpeter, an extreme loner. Man! His music told
stories everyone could feel. And he had a far away look in
his eyes like he had lived inside the life of the song the way
the brothers had. He trembled while he played his 'ax' and
he was 'out of it' for hours after a session. Then there was
Tilman. The boy could blow the hell out of a sax. He was a
credit to any band. He could also think of white vocalists
that felt the vibe but he seemed to be able to connect so
naturally with musicians of color.

'But maybe he was just imagining that and being selfish
with the music', he told himself. Had he become like Gil, an
older bassist that encouraged his playing? Gil had died
about twelve years ago. He was ninety-nine but he disliked
all white musicians playing jazz. Gil remembered when his
mother slapped him in his head for playing jazz and the
white kids in his neighborhood would say, 'liver lips, go
play your nigger music.' It upset him when he saw white
musicians gravitate toward the music that had been
scorned. Anwar could admit that he hadn't really wanted to
share jazz either. He believed black people siphoned the

sound from their souls to assist them in their struggles for liberation and it helped them rescue their identities that had been stolen and silenced by the strange continents they had been scattered upon. Jazz, he felt, was buried deep within his people's necessity to reinvent themselves. It was their 'breathing' music and they loved it deeply, the way it took them to a space and soothed and inspired their minds and souls.

In the passing of years there often emerges an homage that points in the direction of those things once misunderstood, unapproved of things . . . so-called crazed artists, writers, inventors, performers that had been labeled travesties will be revisited and then be referred to as 'geniuses and innovators and forerunners' to a modern world. What was too unique to be understood and accepted will be called '*magnificent*' and ahead of its time then embraced wholeheartedly. This homage had been applied also to jazz. In spite of what the music had been for its inventors, 'fatha time' had made an entranceway for the rest of the world to pass through, sit down and fall in love with the 'song.' Anwar had to accept that the 'secret society' sound had leaked 'out there.' He wasn't exactly sure how he felt about that but he knew one thing for certain, it couldn't be drawn back in.

Chapter 7
Unsolicited Friends

A black couple with two teenagers moved into the complex, right across the hall. This was a kind of extended vacation until their home could be renovated. Anwar had often seen shadows in the hallway through the little space between the bottom of the door and floor. Someone would be standing there listening as he practiced. One Saturday the teenagers knocked on his door and introduced themselves. But he heard an audible sound, like a voice coming from within and around. It was like he was awake but dreaming. Was he becoming schizophrenic? Was this what Buddy had experienced? Was he becoming Buddy? Strangely enough, his bass playing had taken a sudden leap from great to greater. He took a deep breath and as he exhaled, a voice spoke loud and clear, one word only; *DRAMA.*

"What's up, man? This is Demitra, my twin sister," the brother said, giving Anwar a firm handshake.

"I can speak for myself," she asserted. "We're here til our house gets fixed. It caught on fire."

"Oh, a fire," Anwar repeated, very cautiously.

"We play too," the young man said excitedly. "We used to go to a music school in Boston. Oh, my name is Demetrius."

"We gonna enroll in school again as soon as we can move back into our house. Can we sit in and listen to you? We hear you practicing all the time," the young lady added with enthusiasm.

"Look, I just recently got back into my research and—

"Please, please," they begged. 'How would listening to him play hurt anything?' he surmised. So they sat and listened, wiggled their heads from side to side, patted their feet.

They were both tall, nineteen years old, respectful, and full of energy. But both needed to concentrate on their faces that broadcasted their pimply and blotchy skin. A good astringent for a month or two would do the job. When he had gotten to know them better he would mention it.

The twins were good company for Anwar as long as they didn't run their mouths too much. They befriended him and became the nerve wrecking little brother and sister he'd never had. They drank up his soda, ate up his snacks, talked about their dreams and lovers, brought him up to date on the latest dances, tunes and performers. And they idolized him. They were always questioning him about his past appearances and who he had played with. They listened to his stories without a flinch and begged him to 'tell them more.' They followed him to restaurants and he treated them to lunch frequently. He sometimes took them sight seeing, to a lecture or to the library and sometimes to a movie. He learned that Demetrius played a trumpet and Demitra played a saxophone.

"I'm so glad we met you," Demetrius would say when they'd get together. "We can learn from you, man."

The next time their parents went to Boston to get items from storage, the twins went along. They returned with their instruments and showed Anwar what they could do with them, which wasn't much. Finally, and it didn't take long, they had begun to practice with Anwar. He reminded himself to be patient but they were such poor players that it was hard to fathom that they were playing in his living room. He was beyond the point of playing with musicians for the sake of doing music. Those twins would not catch on to anything he showed them. They didn't like to practice and it was quite obvious opportunities to do so evaded them. After they had turned his stomach one day with the pitchy notes and squeals on their horns, he excused himself and rushed into the bathroom to spit up. It turned into ten minutes of uncontrollable retching and coughing.

"You okay, Anwar," they asked, unaware that their music had literally turned his stomach.

"I'm fine," he said, exiting and shutting the bathroom door firmly. "I gotta get out of here and go play."

"Take us with you to a jam session, please!"

"I can't."

"Please? Pretty please?" Demitra pleaded.

"You're not ready. Those musicians are smoking. They'd slaughter you two and make you leave town. You don't practice enough. I never hear you," he said hoping to have ended the subject.

"That's cause our parents say our place is too small," Demitra defended. "It gives them a headache."

"It gives me a headache too," Anwar affirmed. "But you can't let that stop you. You have to find someplace else to practice. You gotta hustle! Hustle!"

"Well we're fine practicing with you," they chanted.

"No! You're messing up my practice time. I'm sorry, but I'm gonna have to throw you two out. After this week, that's it. You have to find someplace else to practice. I need to concentrate."

Anwar didn't want to hurt their feelings but he had been pressed to say something. They were taking his life away. He enjoyed their company at first but he saw they really had nothing to bring to the table and they weren't even serious musicians. He'd seen their type. They'd go home and store their instruments in a small closet and there they would sit until they'd gotten married and had children, then pull out the instruments to show off at a party. It had gotten ridiculous. A top notch musician playing along with beginners? He was hardly arrogant when it came to his music but that just wasn't. . . wasn't right. No. He hadn't come to New Orleans for that. Again, people had somehow gotten all in his mix! He had to put them down. Quickly!

"Why can't we just go with you to one jam session? Take us to just one? Please, Anwar?" they begged.

"Maybe one day. When you're ready. Listen, what are you two doing for your skin?" he finally said without intending to insult anyone.

"What you mean? Wait, wait, wait a minute now. Whoa! What's wrong with our skin?" Demetrius asked defensively?

"It could be a lot clearer, you know? When I was coming up, you were stuck with acne until you grew out of it. Nowadays it can be cured. There's a good dermatologist on—

"I know an insult when I hear one!" Demitra blurted and ran out and slammed the door so hard that his next door neighbor stuck her head into the hallway.

"It's alright," Anwar assured her.

"Well, what happened?" the woman asked nosily.

"It's alright," he said again.

"Well—, I don't know. . . "

"Well, I know. Okay?" Anwar said quickly and shut his door.

"Alright, alright, that's it. Later Demetrius."

"Why do I have to go? Demitra slammed that door."

"Look, I can't be going through this. Your sister got my neighbors all upset and I've got work to do."

"Okay! Okay."

The young man appeared about as forlorn as could be as he put his trumpet away. Anwar began to think that he'd been too hard on them. After all teenagers could be sensitive and especially about their appearance. He'd make it up to them. He'd take them to a jam session. Then, that would be it. They would have to keep to themselves.

"Wait! You don't have to leave, Demetrius. Get your sister and I'll take you two to an open mic with me but just this one time. Check with your parents first. Then I have to get my tunnel vision back. My deadline will be here soon."

"We're going to a jam session? You for real? For real?"

"I'm for real," Anwar said, zipping Bassetta up in her bag. "Go get her."

The twins appeared at his door ready to go in seconds. Anwar didn't take them to the open mic he frequented. He knew they weren't ready for that one but he took them to an open mic in the French Quarters at a club called Chouette Goulet', one of the few that had a parking lot. It was where a lot of amateur talent went. There were some good musicians amongst them but a far cry from the best.

The club was standing room only. It took almost thirty minutes to be served. The twins were very inspired and got visibly antsy every time a musician or singer stepped off the stage.

"I wanna get up there, man. I wanna get up there bad," Demetrius said, bugging Anwar who was sipping on his drink and trying to relax.

"Calm down, man. Your name's on the list. You know what you're gonna play?"

"I'll play anything."

"Look, I know it's an open mic but you can't just get up and play anything. Present yourself as a professional at all times."

"Okay, okay. Me and my sister can play something together. Demitra, remember A-Train?"

"A Train? You two know that?"

"Yeah, we used to practice that all the time," he said as if it were no task.

"I've never heard you practice that," Anwar said with a lot of doubt.

"Well, we can still play it," Demitra said with confidence and a finger snap.

"You have to know that. You can't just jump up there, now. Care about your reputation before you even get one."

"We know. Relax big brother," Demetrius slurred. Then he gave his sister a strange look.

As luck would have it, the MC called the twins names right away.

"Well, the stage is all yours. Do your thing." Anwar said, laughing lightly. 'Boy was this going to be a show'.

In a matter of minutes the twins were on the bandstand. Wouldn't you know it? They took forever to find the right keys in front of everyone then played pitifully. Anwar was really embarrassed because before they left the stage they informed the MC that they were his students and the MC announced it to the audience. Suddenly every halfway decent musician in the club was sniggling at Anwar. The only thing he could do to redeem his dignity was to take Bassetta to the stage. His name was called as soon as the twins stepped down.

He started off with fast melodious plucking and the room grew quiet. When he used his bow a burst of applauses and praises followed and people shouted encouragements. The twins cheered the loudest. After the applause had died down and he was back at the table the twins finally realized they had a lot of serious practice ahead.

"You think you can't do what I did? You can. I can't stress enough how important it is that you practice. You see these people? They practice. It's not a game to them.

Alright, get your things together. I better get you two back."
Anwar downed his drink quickly.

"Why?" Demetrius asked. "Why we have to go back?"

"Because, you're just nineteen, that's why?"

"That's old enough to go to war and get killed, ain't it?"

"Look, end of discussion, man," Anwar said flatly.

"It is," Demetrius added. "Young people can die in war but they can't stay out late. That's cold, man."

"Sure is," Demitra cosigned. "And you won't even let us have a drink. We drank before. A lot of times."

"Well, you only get soda when you're with me. Watch my things while I use the bathroom."

Anwar headed quickly to the men's room. He was glad he didn't have teenagers to raise. 'They could be a pain and a half sometimes', he thought.

The bathroom had only one stall and there were about three men waiting. He would have to wait too. In the meantime, the MC called the next act but that person had apparently left the club. The twins eagerly opted to take that person's place. They quickly unpacked their instruments and began playing a sorry rendition of 'I Remember Clifford.' Anwar couldn't see them but he could hear them and he felt sick on his stomach again. 'They loved choosing difficult songs. That song was worse than the first one. But they enjoyed being seen and maybe that would be their incentive to practice in the future,' he thought. He squirmed and held his breath as he listened to a cacophony of squeaks and sour tones for two and a half minutes. That's all the time the MC gave them, and with good reason.

"Alright, there you have it," the MC interrupted before the twins could slaughter the bridge. "Demetrius and Demitra. They're twins, everybody. Give them a hand. Com' on, you can do better than that."

"But we're not finish," Demetrious said.

"Give them a big hand," the MC said again.

The MC gave a sigh of relief that was heard through the speakers when the twins left the stage. Anwar laughed and shook his head. 'Those kids are a mess,' he thought.

The twins were frenetic when he returned to the table.

"Hey, Anwar! Did you hear us? Did you hear us, man!"

"I heard you," he said to Demetrius whose face was gleaming like a small moon.

"Did you hear me hit that high C?" Demitra asked, still breathing hard. "I did it. I practiced on that."

"Well, good for you. You're coming along. But I also heard a lot of pitchy notes and screeches from both of you. And the MC stopped you. That means you have to practice. Let's get out of here before your parents come after me."

Anwar suddenly jerked and twisted as if he'd been stabbed in his abdomen.

"What's wrong?" the twins asked.

"Where's Bassetta? I left her right here."

"Oh, my God!" Demitra shouted. "Somebody must have taken her when we were playing!"

Something knocked the wind clean out of Anwar. He grabbed hold of the table and breathed hard. The ceiling spun wildly and he hyperventilated to the beat of the music that a guitarist was playing.

"Get my bass," he said, and he was not playing. "I asked you to keep an eye on it. Find my damn, bass!"

The twins scurried about all over the club looking for and asking about Bassetta. Anwar was shaking so badly that he ordered a stiff drink for the road. He knew this was going to be a long night and maybe a rough one but nobody would make love to Bassetta but him.

After inquiring nonstop from the slobbering intoxicated, to the stark and sober, to the refined patrons in the club, they discovered that a tall man, white, or a light-skinned black man had asked who the bass belonged to.

When people said they didn't know, he said he would take it to the manager's office. Anwar checked with the office but it had never been taken there. He was about to explode.

There were a few people hanging around sipping their drinks when the three got outdoors. "Listen," Anwar began. "I will pay any of you for some information. Somebody stole my bass. Did any of you see someone walk out of this club with an upright bass in a soft black bag on wheels? Please, tell me. I'll pay."

The people seemed to feel so sorry for Anwar and Demitra as she cried incessantly.

"I have to—find it. I'm connected to my instrument. Demitra please, dry it up!" But she wouldn't stop crying.

"I saw a man come out with a bass," a young woman said reluctantly. "He got in a van with some other man. I think they were from another country cause I could hear them talking in another language. I saw them go in and they didn't have a bass but I didn't think nothing of it when they came out with one cause I figured maybe they were moving it for someone or maybe they bought it. Wasn't none of my business so I didn't really think too much about it."

"She didn't hear or see nothing," a young man replied. Then under his breath he could be heard saying, "don't get caught up in that shit."

"No, they took this man's instrument," the young lady said while staggering toward Anwar. He need his instrument. For a hundred dollars I'll tell you what kind of van it was."

It was plain to see she was more interested in making 'a dollar' than helping. He knew he was being 'worked' but what could he do? He would pay anything to get Bassetta back. He reached into his wallet reluctantly and slapped a hundred dollar bill in her hand.

"It was a dark green Ford, Windstar."

"Which way did it go?"

"Now that's gonna cost you another two-hundred."

"Aw com'on," Anwar begged. "Don't do me like this."

"Well, I got rent to pay."

"Stop hustling him, Chantal," warned the young man standing beside her.

"Yeah, don't do the brother like that. You wrong, girl," another young man added.

"You gonna pay my rent? Any of yawl? Then shut the fuck up!" she yelled.

She was tough! She was the type that could take on a few men in a fist fight and win.

Two more one-hundred dollar bills were slapped in the young lady's palm. "I didn't see their faces. They wore hoodies. But they went that way," she said pointing. "They turned left at the light. I watched them cause they didn't seem like they belonged in this place. They was too nervous. And the van had a dent on the passenger's side."

In seconds Anwar and the twins were speeding down the road, looking for the van. He was honoring no traffic lights or street signs. In his mind, he could see Bassetta being raped by fingers that had no business touching her. He could see her being scratched and bruised and small children riding her like a broomstick the way Merriam's nephew had tried to do many times. He could hear her giving off sour cries and unable to sing like she could with him and he grew angry that someone would have the audacity to walk out of a club with somebody's instrument.

Buddy. He should have always been focused on Buddy. This had to be karma. There he was with two teenagers that came from out of nowhere and he got caught up in their crap. They were irresponsible. He wouldn't be dealing with them anymore. All he had done for them and he just asked them to keep an eye on his things. People! He was leaving all people alone in New Orleans except Merriam whenever she would come. Of all the things to be dealing with! He could barely think. He just wanted to get Bassetta back and get those twins out of his van, out of his life. He couldn't wait to tell them, 'adios! See ya later. Don't turn around and don't say goodbye. Just go'.

After he'd driven about ten minutes, he saw a dark colored van sitting in a gas station. He could see Bassetta leaning on the back door through the window. There was a man inside and another man on the outside that had just pumped gas into the vehicle. Anwar zoomed into the gas station, running over a median. His van sounded as if it had come apart underneath but he kept going. He jumped out and charged the man head on at the pump. The man put his hands up as though Anwar were a policeman. He had surrendered easily, Anwar thought.

"Okay, okay!" the man said fearfully.

Anwar darted to the passenger's side of the van and yanked on the handle. The door was locked. The man that had been pumping gas jumped into the driver's seat and took off. Anwar ran to his car and took off after him. It was like a chase scene from a movie, up a hill, down a hill, through an alley, sharp turn, hugging a curve, then into a very dark area of the highway. He tried to keep up with them but they obviously knew the road much better than he did and then…they were gone. No signs of them anywhere. He stepped out of the van and looked around in the darkness for a few moments while the twins set as stiff as mannequins. When he climbed back into the car he warned them, "don't say shit to me!" And they didn't.

The tension in the van was so thick it could be eaten. It seemed like hours before they reached the complex. He stopped the twins before they got out and said, "I will be picking you up every morning at seven until I get Bassetta back. You will be my two extra sets of eyes. We're going to look for her everyday and go into every club and any other place I think she could be. If I don't find her, your parents will have to cough up nine-thousand dollars but a new bass can never replace Bassetta. I want you two to understand that. She has been with me for eleven years. We have a bond and furthermore, you have interrupted my research and artistic flow. Those things are priceless." The twins were very broken up as they climbed out of the van. They walked with their heads down as if they carried the weight of the world on their shoulders.

Entering his apartment was like he had gone into a strange warehouse. Things were stored on the shelves but he could relate to nothing. His research seemed unfamiliar, foreign even. After a half-hour or so he called the police and reported Bassetta stolen but he would also have to make a police report at the station.

He didn't remove his clothing that night. He sat curled in a corner shaking and unable to sleep. He glanced at his watch about every three minutes. Finally around five in the morning he dozed off but he was up again at seven. He didn't wash or eat. He blew the horn for the twins and they all headed to the police station, then they went riding around searching for and asking about Bassetta until almost three in the morning. This went on for almost two weeks. Anwar's research came to a complete halt. He stopped eating, started losing weight, stopped shaving and some-times his electrolytes were so low his hands trembled. He even cried over Bassetta once and cringed to think he would have to replace her. Finally, he began eating but his daily meals consisted of corn chips, McDonalds and coffee. The twins barely ate too and had to eventually tell their parents why they were spending so much time with Anwar. Their parents assured Anwar that they would replace Bassetta if she couldn't be found.

Somewhere in the middle of a vestibule, an illegitimate office, in the back of a shabby club, sat five men counting and fussing over money. Instruments sat against a wall awaiting a new home. The two white men Anwar had chased, Nardo and Cappi, were there donning new clothes and smoking skinny cigars like they were men of stocks and bonds. Being white, clubs security didn't question the instruments they carried out. They spoke with two other men, one black, Shorty, and one white, Billups, head honchos of the villainous theft ring. Another man was there, Red Crown, called just 'Crown,' Shorty's nephew. He was under twenty-five and more in the way than helpful. Shorty had made a promise to his dying sister that he would keep her son employed. He hadn't told her how though.

Shorty and Billups started the organized theft ring when they discovered the value of musical equipment and instruments. Their responsibilities had been to enter, scope the clubs, assess the value of the instruments and equipment and assign Nardo, Cappi and Crown the task of going inside and removing any unattended things of value. Thus, leaning against the wall in the back alley office were amplifiers, guitars, cellos, all types of horns and flutes, congo drums and Bassetta.

A pile of bills sat in the middle of the table and Shorty grabbed a handful and began to deal them as though they were a deck of playing cards. First the hundreds were passed out, then the fifty's, then the twenty's, the tens, the fives, the singles and the change was thrown into a vase for the purchasing of odds and ends. The men had made out well, especially Shorty and Billups who were presented with a large percentage of what the instruments brought because Shorty supplied the space to store the stolen goods, while Billups supplied the transportation to deliver them.

"Grab that bass and take it out front," Shorty demanded of Crown who sat hypnotized by the music flowing from his headphones. "An' what I tell you about wearing those things when we doin' business? Take em off."

Crown did as his uncle had requested and moved slowly towards Bassetta, feeling lost and awkward without his music. He didn't appear to have the personality for the job he had been assigned. Stealing? No way. He had a dreamy look in his eyes as though he were in love or was a poet.

"Hurry up. Nobody got all day."

The young man grabbed Bassetta and wheeled her into the sitting area of the club and leaned her against the wall.

New Orleans had many crevices, each with its own dignifying stamp. Some wore bright neon marquees that were adorned in warm invitations for those who were new or simply browsing in the area. Some crevices gave off an eerie secluded message much like the old 'red light' districts had done years earlier, warning visitors that they had entered at their own risk. One such particular crevice greeted Anwar and the twins. It was called 'The Nook.' The three looked one another in the faces as if they would never see each other again after entering the dilapidated structure. The small moist and rotting wooden building that doubled as a warehouse for stolen instruments and equipment, blended perfectly with the darkness while a single piercing light above it ordained the path of broken cobblestones which would eventually lead to a small foyer filled with mostly beer drinking customers who snapped their fingers and sang to old soul music. Anwar and the twins made their way into what was called the 'bubble,' a rotunda with a stage that was propped with unattended instruments and equipment. Stained, violet colored drapes covered a peeling and cracked wall. The thirteen inch surplus was turned into a mat for musicians to wipe their feet of the parking lot's grime and gravel. The room smelled of beer and arm pits.

"It stinks in here," Demitra said with the malice and arrogance of a millionaire's daughter being dropped off at an overcrowded bus station.

"Deal with it," Anwar returned, indifferently.

"Man this ain't no place to be," Demetrius squalled.

"You know why we're here? *Do you know why we're here*?" Anwar snapped apathetically and interrogating them more than asking. "We're here cause somebody let a man walk up and take my bass. Don't dismiss that, please. And don't make me lose my temper. Matter of fact, just wait in the van. Please!"

"Thank God," Demitra blurted, holding her breath and walking away quickly.

Anwar strolled to another end of the club and headed for the bartender who had no idea his boss was involved in a scheme that left musicians miserable and unemployed.

"Has anyone come in here to sell an upright bass?" He asked.

Expecting a 'no,' he was knocked off his feet when the young bartender said, "you don't mean this one, do you? Crown just sat it here. I can go to the back and get him if you want me to."

"No, I mean this one, yes, it's mine's already. Somebody stole it. Who's Crown?"

"Whoa. Hey I only been working here for three weeks. I ain't involved in nothing. But I've been getting a bad feeling about this place. Somebody need to check out that backroom. That's all I'm gonna say. But I ain't supposed to know about that, okay? I can't be getting in no trouble. I came to New Orleans to shoot a movie."

"Well, I'm gonna call the police," Anwar stated firmly.

"Ay man, do what you have to do. I quit."

He removed his apron and stood off to the side of the bar. He looked pitiful as though the job had been a vital part of his livelihood. After a few minutes, he said to Anwar, "hey, this is New Orleans. I'll find something else. They were underpaying me anyway."

Anwar's heart had climbed into his throat. He had found Bassetta. He would know her bag anywhere. The men he had chased came out of the room and took a seat at a table as though they were waiting for someone. Anwar quickly went outside with a bounce to his step. The twins knew something was up.

"You find her?"

"Yeah, just stay in the car."

He looked around the parking lot until he located the green Ford, Windstar. He took out a pocketknife and slashed all four tires, this time making sure the men couldn't get away. He reentered the club to wait on the police *but* being Anwar, he had to take matters into his own hands.

He thought about how hard he had worked and saved to buy Bassetta during his last few years of college. It was his right to take what he owned he concurred. But first he sat beside the taller man and humored him.

"You play bass?"

"What? Bass? I donta play. You wanta bass? You buy?"

"I bought bass."

"Oh. You donta need another?"

"No. Because this is the one I bought and this is the one I'm taking. You remember me? You stole this from me at the Chouette Goulet'. Well, I'm taking it back."

Anwar rose slowly and suddenly began thinking about the twins. He didn't want to put them in danger and hoped they would stay in the car. But he was taking Bassetta back at all costs. The bartender made gestures for him to stop, trying to warn him that what he was doing was dangerous. Of course he ignored him. The shorter man reached into his pocket like a man would do that had a weapon. This,

Anwar had not anticipated. He backed up to the bar. The man reached for Basetta and unfolded an old fashioned straight razor. Unexpectedly, the man was bombarded by several black male patrons, each shouting threatening words and obscenities and yelling for him to put the blade down. Anwar's back was arched across the bar as the man held the razor to his throat, demanding that he release Bassetta. That is when the man was tackled and his face held down on the floor until he dropped the blade. He got up and broke out running. Red Crown followed.

That had been Anwar's second account with danger. But the brothers had been on his side this time.

"Man, you had already called the police. You shoulda just chilled. Now they got away," the bartender said, in a disgusted tone.

"They won't get far without wheels," Anwar smirked.

A musician with an electric guitar appeared from a side entrance. The scent of marijuana reeked from his clothing and some people fanned the air with their hands. He saw Anwar with Bassetta and with a friendly demeanor asked "what's up with the bass, man? I was gonna to buy it."

"It's mine. Those men stole it. It's not for sale, man!"

"You serious? They stole it? Those white men? Sheet—, that's crazy man. They know where they at? They don't know where they at, do they bro?"

"Man, you lucky, no lie. You lucky," the ex-bartender said repeatedly. "Ey, I'm outta here. I just came to New Orleans to make a movie, that's all." He didn't search for the boss to get his pay and he didn't say goodbye. He just stepped out and kept walking.

The three men had jumped into the van and tried to pull off but they had only gone a few yards before a rim buckled and the van went down. They were then met by the police. The men told the police Bassetta belonged to the shorter man and Anwar had tried to steal it so they all had to go down to the police station. Anwar worried that the police might believe the white men over him even though he gave a detailed description of Bassetta, including her nicks and scratches. He had also thought to bring a copy of Bassetta's purchase receipt with him. If that wouldn't be proof enough, he would play her.

After two hours Bassetta was released to him and the men were thrown in jail, including poor dreamy Crown.

Demetrius helped put Bassetta into the van while Demitra laughed and clapped and said 'hallelujah' repeatedly. Anwar took a few seconds to hug Bassetta as though he were hugging a child that had been rescued from its abductors. The twins apologized and stroked Bassetta's bag but Anwar was angry, visibly angry, where he rolled his eyes and threw up his hands whenever they started to speak.

"I got her back but you're not off the hook. You got a scolding coming! You couldn't watch my stuff? You had to play that bad that you couldn't look out for me? All I've done for you? That's selfishness. You know what this bass means to me?" The twins didn't respond. They sat in silence until they reached the complex. They did not show their faces at Anwar's door for three weeks and that was when they went to tell him goodbye. They were returning to Boston. They apologized for being irresponsible and promised him that they would practice more.

"Yeah, yeah, do that and maybe one day I'll come to see you at Carnegie Hall. Take care of yourselves."

He hugged them and shook their hands and they were off. He felt relieved. No sentimental bonds there. No exchange of phone numbers, nothing. He felt absolutely nothing. He had almost lost Basetta because of them. He'd never owned a bass with her tone and touch. She had made him a star on many stages. He loved young folks but hanging out with them would not happen again, not for a long time. He crossed over to Bassetta and stroked her gently then leaned forward and kissed her passionately. He wondered if other musicians loved their instruments enough to kiss them or was he just plain crazy? But then he thought of Jimi Hendrix. Of course, Jimi kissed his instrument. That's Jimi. If Jimi did it then it's ordained and who is anyone to question it? He leaned over and kissed Bassetta again, twice. Then he fixed himself a cup of tea and called Merriam to tell her he had found Bassetta. No more would he let people walk on his path. He was in New Orleans for Buddy and nothing else. Damn all those strangers. Yeah. He finally got a good night's sleep.

As the warm weather shied away to coolness, he did a little more research for Giles and put it into a very impressive format. By the time he had compiled all the information, it had began to look like a small book. That would be enough. Giles would think he'd been working like crazy and if he didn't think that, it was a heck of a whole lot more than what the other professors had returned with.

He started researching Buddy again. Every day, every hour, and every moment, he researched something about Buddy. Those teenagers had only been a distraction. They brought nothing, absolutely nothing to the table. Just burned his time up. Yep, he was going to just keep to himself and focus on Buddy. The only person he would call besides Merriam was Giles, not to chat but just to check in with him. He'd bring him up to date on his research and plans then go right back to work.

Chapter 8
Ridicule

He'd began to interview people again. Some of them found his work fairly interesting. There were those who loved nothing more than socializing with him for the sake of indulging in deep discussions about jazz or entering into long debates over musicians and composers. In the end they would both learn something new. But then, it was that small handful of people who were adamant on making things difficult . . . *for him.*

New Orleans was comprised of several provinces and areas that were sectioned off much like New York City. Each had its own personality, pulse and energy, appearing to be self-operated, not even a part of the city. Anwar enjoyed discovering remote little areas as such. Those places were often rough and raw, highly populated and urbanized. Buddy had romped around in those spots. Anwar would take pictures of the surroundings with little regard to whom he might have captured in the shot or whomever he may have interrupted. Oftentimes he posed to capture an image right in the middle of two people having a conversation. He hadn't always excused himself either and that put a bitter wall between him and many of the residents. Once a man pushed him out of the center of his group's conversation right into the street and remarkably he missed getting hit by a bus. Truthfully, he had developed a sense of entitlement before he even arrived in the City. He had the arrogance of a paparazzi who was never there for the people but instead for what he could gain for himself. Whenever he had gotten a sneer from the people he sneered them back, not realizing he was the intruder and was *alone*. He had gone to a pretty run down area, predominantly black. The moment he climbed out of his car, he was ridiculed.

"Yeah, look at this niggah," a tough oldster said. "Here he come with a damn notebook. Now just what the hell he want?"

Three men, apparently good friends, looked in each other's faces and nudged one another in the shoulder or midriff with their elbows as Anwar approached them, a secret language they had all apparently understood. They had probably enjoyed doing to others many times what they were prepared to do to Anwar. With arms crossed and legs spread wide as though blocking him from an entranceway to a forbidden world, they started their shit.

"We don't want none and leave us alone," the shortest man yelled.

"That's where you're wrong gentlemen," Anwar quickly defended. "I'm not a salesman. I heard this is where I could find someone that knew King Buddy Bolden."

All of the men burst out laughing. Finally one man stopped laughing long enough to speak.

"Ain't nobody living that knew Buddy Bolden. You crazy?" He began laughing again.

With his pen out and ready to scribble down a name, Anwar realized he must have sounded ridiculous.

"Buddy died almost seventy yars ago," one man added.

"That mean somebody dat knew him woulda had to be least a good hundred and ten cause ya gotta count da yars Buddy spent in da crazy house. When you think Buddy was born? I know he was born in 1877. Jazz is my thang and I studied him."

"Wow, what am I thinking," Anwar said, feeling very foolish. "I meant to ask, 'do you know anyone that had known somebody else that had known Buddy'."

"Ya lookin' right at em. Alla our people roun' here that knew Buddy is daid but my great grandfatha talked to him and gave him a buttin' offa his unifoam the day his band marched. Say he knew Buddy was gonna play different."

"Oh yeah? Tell me, how old—

"Whacha wan' all dis information fo'?" the shorter man blurted.

"I'm a jazz researcher for a college. My department needs it for the textbook it's preparing."

"What kinda college? Black?"

"Well—umh . . . mixed," he lied.

"Well las' time somebody come roun' asking questions, it was a white man and my mama talked to him and din he come out wit some kinda doc'ment and my mama was outdone. She say he fancied up huh words an' turned dem roun' and she hadn't said none of that. So we don't like to tell nothing now."

"An how we know you ain't gwonna jes run off and take what we tell ya to da white man?" the tallest one asked.

"We don't trus' Negroes like you. You wear white men's shoes," another added.

"No. . . they're just shoes that are made to last," Anwar defended.

"Well, black folks roun' here wouldn't be caught daid in em. Mean you must 'dentify wit' the white man."

"That's not true. But if you don't want to tell me anything, do you know somebody who will?"

The three men grinned as Anwar spoke, a playful gleam in their eyes. They took a deep breath in unison and released a great big "HELL NOOOO!!!" A burst of laughter followed.

The next few months were all the same. No information. Those that had it wouldn't give it and some that gave it didn't have it. Like one man had claimed to be the great grandson of a woman who had secretly given birth to his grandmother, a child he claimed Buddy had fathered. He wanted to know if he would receive part of the royalties when the textbook had been written. Anwar responded, "sure my man. All you have to do is prove it. Bring us your grandmother's birth certificate with Buddy's name on it as the father."

"Forget it then," the man huffed. "I ain't got to prove my descent to nobody. I know who I am!"

There were others who gave information freely but it had not been helpful. He was getting desperate. It seemed like a conspiracy not to give him any information about Buddy. He even spoke with jazz aficionados at a symposium at Tulane University to discuss the development of jazz. He stood to introduce himself in the large lecture room.

"My name is Anwar Rasual, I'm a performing musician, a bassist to be exact and a professor. I'm in New Orleans on sabbatical to research past marching bands and to find relics belonging to Buddy Bolden, specifically something regarding his music, like his cylinder. I'd be very appreciative for information or assistance any of you can offer. Thank you."

The moderator, a black female professor, sat one row in front of Anwar. She made a *'tsk'* sound and turned around, glanced at Anwar's nametag and began telling him that researching Buddy was not beneficial. An argument ensued and it was pretty heated. She spoke loudly, intentionally embarrassing him.

"Mr. Rasual, a cylinder? Are you serious? **People, he's here looking for Buddy's cylinder. Can you believe? How foolish.**" Some attendees agreed with her and shook their heads and stared at Anwar.

Anwar was steaming. She had made mockery of his mission to a room of over two-hundred attendees. "I will not allow you to reduce my passion to mockery because you do not share my mission and see things only from your perspective," Anwar defended.

"Oh really? My perspective? Mr. Rasual, I just want to know why you are wasting your time researching a jazz ghost? A cylinder? Please! People have been looking for Buddy's cylinder ever since he was committed in the early 1900's. That should tell you something. They're gone, stolen or whatever!"

"Or they haven't been discovered, *yet!*" Anwar said, hoping to rekindle respect of his mission from the others.

"This is a symposium to discuss the development. . . development of jazz, Mr. Rasual. Let me make that clear. We have fresh new talent now or have you noticed? Research those people and put them on the map. Buddy had his turn," she said, wobbling her head all the while.

"Buddy spent 24 years locked away while other people tore through his collection and helped themselves. People literally stole his music. I don't consider that having a turn."

Anwar knew he had responded without tact as he sometimes did because the attendees sniggled at him. They raised their brows in anticipation of the argument increasing momentum and intelligent words changing into insulting comments and accusations, even profanity.

"But you're overlooking the evolvement of jazz," the woman continued. "Jazz moves on. Don't stunt its growth by picking up a dead piece of it and trying to shake it alive. It's gone. We thank Buddy for what he gave us but now we have to move on. Move on, Mr. Rasual. And please don't take this personally but you seem so passionate, like you are Buddy. Are you his incarnate?"

"First of all, ma'am, I do take this very personal and as far as I'm concerned every black jazz musician in America is Buddy's incarnate. And so are you but maybe you just don't understand. Or maybe you don't have the historical information to put it all together to understand."

"Right. I'm an idiot. I don't understand."

"Idiot? If the shoe fits, then wear it. But I'll tell you what *I don't understand*—I don't understand you so-called black musical intellectuals leaving your roots behind." He looked accusingly at the fifty-percent of black persons in attendance. Again eyebrows were raised.

"No, you're just obsessed. I reiterate, you're possessed, Mr. Rasual," she continued, "and we are not interested," she screamed.

"What gives you the right to speak for the others here?" Anwar snapped.

"Is anybody else here running around this city looking for a Buddy Bolden cylinder?" she asked the attendees. No one spoke up. Instead there was laughter. Some people held their notebooks up and laughed behind them. Others ducked beneath counter desks and laughed. "There you have it. Nobody! You're stuck in the past with Buddy," she retorted. "Face it!"

People shook their heads and whispered to one another and some were so tickled that they couldn't catch their breaths. A gathering of the city's most respected jazz researchers, musicians, and vocalists went from a sophisticated forum of like minded academicians to a distasteful shouting match and Anwar was a qualifying opponent. He gathered his notebook and other items.

"This symposium has been a waste of my time. I am absolutely shocked at the level of disrespect we have for our history and ancestors. Good afternoon to everyone." He disappeared through the huge double doors.

The woman continued, "why is it that these days we can't even have an intelligent discussion? He walks out. And I wouldn't give him Buddy's cylinder if I found it, would you? Who does he think he is?" People agreed with her. "We only have five minutes before break. Let's do that now. There's coffee in the next room."

'A lot of those professors had unwittingly tried to belittle me because that tyrant coached them on,' he thought. He desperately wanted something of Buddy's to shut their mouths. He needed a creation or something right away that represented Buddy. He had to prove that Buddy Bolden was more than a legendary memoir to do guesswork on. But whatever items of Buddy's that had been discovered were in museums and not all of them were very significant. His heart felt heavy to think that no one in the jazz world had ever heard Buddy's music. Buddy, some researchers claimed, hadn't written his music out, and some of the musicians that heard it and had written it out, may not have written it in the context that Buddy had played it. 'It had been documented that Buddy had indeed recorded on wax cylinders so why not search for them?' Some historians had determined that the cylinders couldn't have survived. 'What do they know?' Anwar thought, as he peeled the nametag label off his sports coat and balled it up. Just because they hadn't found the cylinder didn't mean it didn't exist. Cylinders as old as Buddy's had survived and the music had been duplicated and circulated. So just maybe somewhere in the city was one of Buddy's cylinders. But where? He needed a clue badly. Was he just wasting his time? Was he too tendentious? Was he obsessed? Or was he *possessed*? The anger returned when he thought about how the woman ridiculed him.

"Excuse me, excuse me, sir." A masculine voice prodded its way into Anwar's private moment in the corridor of the lecture hall. He turned around slowly and realized a whole heap of anger had turned around with him.

When one is angry there is a primordial thudding that starts from the chest and works its way to the head producing an intense heat that pulsates like a heartbeat. Until the heat digresses, there is no point trying to communicate with the subject for surely there will be confrontation. This, the strange man that had approached Anwar, understood. He leaned on the mahogany railing of the granite stairs as Anwar struggled to regain his composure breathing in and out like Merriam had shown him when she had taken a meditation class. He stood facing the man who was nearly his height. He was glaring at him like a bull facing a meddlesome matador but the man wasn't intimidated. He continued to stand patiently. Finally the anger leaked out to who knows where and he was able to speak and think normally again.

"What is it?" Anwar asked. He recognized the man as one of the professors that had been in the room. Had he been on the woman's side too?

"Listen, I am so sorry they came down on you like that. You didn't deserve it. People have a right to their passions. But I'd like to talk to you a minute."

"If it's to talk me out of researching Buddy, I'm not interested."

"Oh, like I said, people have a right to their passions and she was way out of line to do that to you but Shavonne is confrontational with everyone. Every forum or workshop she has run has ended up like this, so don't feel bad about what happened but in all honesty, you shouldn't have let her take you there."

"What can I say? That was my first time meeting her."

"And hopefully, it will be your last. She invented the word, 'killjoy.' I'm headed to the student lounge to meet my wife. It's not too far away. We can talk there. Oh, I'm Ron Dawson. I'm actually a musicologist and I never miss out on an opportunity to discuss jazz. I think the lounge is to the right."

"I'm Anwar Rasual."

He and Ron shook hands and made their way to the cafeteria. They ordered coffee and donuts then claimed a table adjacent to the door.

"Is your wife a musicologist too?"

"No, actually she's a dialectologist."

"Oh, well she should have a great time in this city. I've heard about five different dialects already."

"She's counted eleven and you'd better believe she's having a great time with the history here. She's on sabbatical to write her next book."

"So am I. I'm here to research early jazz bands. *Allegedly.*"

"I know what that means." They laughed and Anwar relaxed a little more.

"Now listen, when I heard you mention Buddy, I immediately thought of my wife. Her research leads her to all kinds of cylinders. The earliest dialog appeared on them, not discs. It's fascinating to watch her work but she happens to know practically every recording company that made cylinders. I thought you might be interested in that. There's also something else but I think I'll let her talk to you about that."

"Okay. I'll be glad to hear it. Anything that will help is what I'm looking for. Anything. In fact, I'm desperate."

Both men peered around at the large opening leading to the corridor and several other departments. The school was huge and prestigious, one of New Orleans greatest assets.

"This university takes me back to my old school days," Anwar admitted. "Looking at those kids makes me glad I'm not a student anymore. I remember one word very well in school, struggle. But I brought it on myself. My father would send money and I'd spend it up on music."

"Yeah," Ron said. "Those were the days of hard knocks for me too. Did ya party a lot? Musicians usually do."

"No, not at all. I was a serious student, very focused. I was a geek until I graduated and started traveling. But when I was in school I practiced about ten hours a day. I played until the wee a.m. Like I said, I play bass. After I graduated, people would come up to me and say things like, 'don't you remember me? I sat next to you all semester.' I had no idea who was who."

"Wow. I thought you might have been a real extrovert. You sort of have that look."

"Oh? Well I'm more social now than I was back then."

"Well, I got focused when I got to grad school. Under-grad was an embarrassing blotch in my life. That's when I met my wife. Shortly after that I learned there was something called 'academic probation." Again the men laughed. "But my wife didn't let romance cramp her style. Do you find that women can be very focused?" Anwar gave him a shrug of the shoulder. "Well, I do. Just watch them."

Suddenly, there were very faint footsteps. A cute, fairly petite lady, about thirty-five donning a shaved head and huge loop earrings, made her way down the corridor leaning terribly from the weight of an oversized bag and a little rough boy. She struggled to keep the child folded in her arms while he struggled for an opportunity to turn the beautiful corridor into a running track. Which one would win? The child was obviously very strong.

"Sudan, stop it now. Stop it. You're not getting down. Here. Here's keys." She gave the child her bundle of keys but they did very little to hold his attention. Ron heard the footsteps and froze a second or two as he put his listening skills to work.

"That sounds like my wife now. You know you've been married too long when you can recognize your wife's footsteps." The men got another good laugh and Ron rose to meet his wife at the entrance. The child had wiggled so badly until his mother practically held him by his feet alone.

"Whoa, hey buddy, straighten up. What did I say?"

Like magic the little boy did as his father demanded. 'A father plays an important role,' Anwar thought.

"Jolene didn't show up. Every since she made college cheerleader she's been putting her babysitting job last. She could have at least called. I had to take him with me to the meeting on the bus. Can you believe that?" Ron's cute little wife explained.

"We're going to just have to find somebody else. It's no big deal. Come here, hon. I want you to meet someone."

He grabbed the little boy, sat him upon his shoulders and headed back to the table. Anwar imagined he and Merriam with a little boy, small and cute like the couple had and he grew sad and remorseful. The past had cut its way into the present and he had a good anxiety attack that triggered an outpour of perspiration that ran down his back and into his pants.

"Anwar, this is my wife, Ashanti."

"Pleased to meet you, Anwar," she said in a high pitched tone.

Ron pulled a chair out for her then took a seat with his son still on his shoulders. After a few moments he placed the little boy on his lap.

"Your son has been showing out everywhere and has given me the blues. Pure indigo," she sighed.

"It's all my fault," Ron confessed, jokingly. "He's already so smart that he thinks he's grown and can do as he pleases. I used to spend almost two hours a day reading to him and teaching him ABC's and how to count and do math. This was while he was still in the womb! I've read that that's where the brain really gets a head start. Say hi to Anwar, son."

The child who was obviously not much older than two and a half spoke amazingly well.

"Hello Anwar, my name is Sudan."

The little boy extended his tiny hand and Anwar shook it. It felt soft, clammy and frangible and the boy reminded him of Merriam's nephew.

"He's a handful and we're having another one," Ashanti said, rubbing her stomach.

"Congratulations," Anwar said, *possibly* with a little envy.

"I'm almost scared to teach this next one," Ron laughed. "No, I'm going about it the same way I did with Sudan but we're in a dilemma. My little man's teachers want him to be placed in advanced classes. Com' on, for God's sake, he's still in nursery school! We don't know if we should give him over to a world of academics and technology that would rob him of his childhood or not."

"That's a tough one," Anwar agreed. "If you hold him back, he won't grow and if you let him go, he'll be forever inundated with books and computers. That's not a bad world, just not a good world for a child."

"Exactly," Ron answered, then turned to his wife.

"Honey, Anwar came to New Orleans to do research. He's looking for Buddy Bolden's cylinder."

"And whatever else I can find of his," Anwar interjected.

Ashanti perked up quickly and said dreamily, "I love Buddy Bolden. Oh would you listen to me going on like I knew him personally. But he's a great legend around here. People are still infatuated with who he was. I've heard so many things about him. They say he went insane because he was playing the devil's music."

Anwar took offense to that. He thought it was strange that people were still spreading that rumor after so many years. "If it had been the devil's music, I think I would be insane by now too, believe me," he told Ashanti.

"Oh, I know it's just folklore. But it's still exciting to consider it. I think the mystery surrounding him is what intrigues people. And tell me this, was he really a pimp?"

"I doubt it. He was too in love with music to waste his time pimping." Ashanti was very inquisitive and Anwar felt like an expert as she questioned him about Buddy.

"Hon listen," Ron said, stopping her firing away of the questions. "Where is the best place for him to look for Buddy's cylinder?"

"Now that's going to be a task. Are you sure it exists?"

"Some researchers says it doesn't exist but that's because they haven't discovered it yet."

"I get you. Assumptions. I hate assumptions. Okay. Well, some recording companies traveled to the south frequently to record talent at that time. I know Columbia and Victor did and they may have even formed small subsidiaries to market and record local music. Buddy was a local talent so he may have been recorded by a smaller company. There's just no way to know. What year was he committed into the asylum?"

"In 1907."

"So we're looking for a company operating before that time. It could be a subsidiary or a major. And if it was a major company they might have taken the finished product with them because Buddy was such an innovator. Hopefully, it was a local company because you'd have a better chance finding the cylinders. But then there's another variable. Buddy may have gone out of town to make the recording. We're talking more than likely, New York."

"New York! Oh, this is discouraging."

"Don't be discouraged. My work gets really tedious when I can't find a recording company or publisher but I never give up and a few months ago I hit the jackpot. I mean a real jackpot."

"Tell him how long you were searching for the oldest recorded black dialog," Ron said with a proud grin."

"Eight grueling years. Nearly everyday and all over the country. I looked so hard until our marriage was suffering."

"That's too much information, hon. Tell him how you found the recordings."

"Ron, we don't know that for sure."

"We do, I do. Go on, tell him."

"Well, Ron tends to think—that Marie Laveau helped.

"Hey, Anwar. . ., I know she did."

"I only know a little about her," Anwar confessed.

"Everything they say is true," Ron blurted.

"Ron, come on now. We just don't know," said Ashanti, giving her husband an ominous scowl. "Yes, she was New Orleans voodoo queen. She was very powerful and millions of people still visit her tomb. And she was a very kind woman in real life but folklore says she was wicked or put spells on people and all; but the only thing we know for sure is that she was an herbalist, a healer, and she helped a lot of people get well. Maybe she resorted to using ritual from time to time, I don't know but she was a panacea for people in this city, especially poor people. Some people swear she manipulated things for the better in their lives."

"Tell him what happened, honey."

"Well, I visited her tomb and made a wish that I would discover the oldest recorded black dialog and my boss called me the next day and needed me to go to Virginia immediately for an assignment, which I did but I fooled around and sprung my ankle getting off the plane. I thought it was fractured—

"And she goes to the doctor when she's in Virginia and while she's at the doctor an upholsterer goes to that same office to fit and measure cloth for the chairs in the waiting area. That was no coincidence . . . well, they get to talking and the lady tells her she has recordings of her ancestors interviews on cylinders at her house and that they've been in the family as long as she could remember—

"He won't even let me tell my story," she interrupted.

"You take too long."

"So what, it's my story. He has to have the details."

"No he doesn't. Look, to make a long story short, the lady gives her the cylinders and they were just what she was looking for. They turned out to be recordings of the oldest black dialog in America," Ron chuckled.

"So far, Ron."

"There's nothing older. I have faith. And this happened three days after she asked Marie Laveau to help her. That's not coincidental. That was Marie Laveau or the universe but definitely something stronger than man. Look how everything was orchestrated just so. But only after she visited Marie Laveau." Ron paused to give his begging son a piece of a donut. "The universe is on Queen Marie's side."

"That can't be instantiated but I don't even question it anymore. I just say thank you, to whomever," Ashanti added, tossing up her arms wildly.

"Well," Ron said, "I thought about you in the meeting and felt you would be a good candidate for Marie LaVeau."

"Three days? After eight years? Well, I am desperate to say the least. So I've just got one question for you two. Where the hell is her tomb?"

"See baby, I knew he was open minded and we need to get out of not wanting to let people know we believe in our ancestor's power. I'm not ashamed. Frankly, I'm ashamed that at one time I didn't believe. We believe in everybody else's ancestors and their religions, and holidays but don't believe our own," Ron added dramatically. "That's crazy," he added, holding his son a little tighter.

"I can't get over that. Three days? I'm thinking about all the fortuitous actions like how you were sent to Virginia and how you were made to spring your ankle to get you to that doctor. Now *you know* that wasn't a coincident. Then, at the perfect timing, a woman who has the cylinder in her possession shows up at the office you're in. She could have gone anywhere in the country but she showed up at *that* office at *that* time. I think Marie Laveau orchestrated that too. Without a doubt," Anwar concluded.

"Marie Laveau," Ron repeated. "Our ancestors were powerful. They left their energy with us. Buddy left energy too. Look how many people still dig jazz. That's nothing but energy. And get this: we were trying to have another baby for two years. We wanted to have our kids close together. We couldn't get pregnant. We went to several doctors and nothing, right baby? They didn't know why."

"It's simple. One of us wasn't working, that's why," she said with a giggle. "But I asked Marie Laveau to help me conceive while I was there too. Less than two weeks later, I was pregnant." She patted her stomach softly.

"She's a powerful sister, Anwar. If I were you, I would go see her today. But they say everybody won't get their desires right away. I'm told Marie Laveau grants them when she feels the person is ready and has learned what they need to know. But if I were you brother, I wouldn't waste another minute talking about it."

"Well, I feel a little ridiculous but I'm ready." Anwar downed his coffee, doubting but hoping Marie Laveau would work in his life quickly. "I'd like to go now. How do I get there?"

"Ashanti knows the way."

"I'll ride out there but I don't need to go see her again. She would probably say I'm being greedy. But we'd better hurry up. The cemetery closes at three and we'll have to drop Sudan off at my friend's." The little boy was almost asleep. His head rested comfortably against his father's chest. Before they left he was snoring.

Ashanti forgot to tell the men how far they had to walk after they had parked. And surprisingly, there were hundreds of people still making their way toward the tomb, all of them hoping they would be granted what they desired.

"We'll get there, don't worry. I have cigars and liquor for her too. They're like my offering for what she did for me. Some people mark an 'x' on her grave but I wouldn't want to deface it. I spun around three or four times and knocked on her tomb. I'm not sure but I think I told her what I wanted after that, not before. I came here when it was raining and not too many people were out. I caught the sniffles behind it but I was holding onto sanity by a piece of thread and it was all worth it."

They were inching their way to the cemetery, talking about the likes of three professors who are supposed to be logical and learned and at the same time rooted in African ritual. They concurred that voodoo had been part of a culture that was stolen from them and should at least be investigated, never scorned and shunned like it had been done for centuries. People came from all over the world to visit the great voodoo queen. 'And why had some people visited her every year? Could it be she still had power?'

They remained steadfast, inch by inch, nearing the grave of the woman that had taught people that death had no end. Inch by inch, they spoke amongst themselves. Ashanti mentioned sabbatical, Ron mentioned North Carolina and Anwar mentioned Merriam and Bassetta. Inch by inch . . .

It was exactly three o'clock when they learned the exhibit had closed. They made a fuss that everyone heard.

"I don't believe it. All this trouble and we can't get in." Ron huffed and grunted but soon calmed down. "Okay, we'll have to come back tomorrow and we'll come early."

"I can't come tomorrow. You know I have that workshop," Ashanti reminded her husband.

"Well, we can come ourselves. We know where it is now. Can you come back, Anwar?" Ron asked.

Anwar didn't answer. He was wondering if there was any way he could to get to the tomb that day.

Two young men approached with the demeanor of skilled salesmen. They looked like brothers. One was obviously older. They appeared to be a mixture of black and Native American, perhaps Creole. They had overheard the three's conversation. Felt their discontent.

"Excuse me," one led off, "it's plain to see that you really want to get in. You probably live out of town, right? You probably have a tight schedule and can't get back, right? You probably didn't expect to see a line like this, right?"

Ashanti listened to them intently then whispered proudly to Ron and Anwar, "I know the exact area these guys are from."

They both were fast talkers, the younger faster than the older one. "People, we know you have been waiting for hours to see New Orleans powerful Voodoo Queen, the one who has healed the sick, the one who has answered thousands of questions, the one who has made so many broken hearts well again, the one and only, Marie Laveau." The young man drew closer and whispered, "we can get you in for a small fee."

"What kind of fee?" Anwar inquired, eagerly.

"Well, I can tell you it's a small cost for a life changing opportunity," the oldest fellow replied. "Our voodoo queen has literally changed the lives of millions of people and can change yours too. If you want to see her, come back tonight at nine. It will only cost twenty-five dollars apiece."

"Twenty-five dollars? That's a rip off!" Ron said. "How could you do people like that? Let's get out of here."

"Fifteen dollars?" the younger brother blurted before they could turn back."

"No, we're not interested. Are you, Anwar? The tomb's not going anywhere," Ron added. "We can come back."

Anwar thought a few seconds then regurgitated the street wisdom he had developed while he had been on the road. 'Talk them down,' he thought.

"We can come back, tomorrow. So why would we pay fifteen dollars to see her tonight? If you were talking five dollars we would take you up on your offer, but not fifteen. Let's get out of here," he said to the couple.

The younger fellow's lips turned into a thin tight line. He was obviously disgusted at the offer but felt something was better than nothing. "Wait. You said five? Okay, we're taking a loss because actually my brother is putting his freedom on the line. He's a master electrician and—

His brother wasn't happy about him exposing his role in the scheme. "Hey man, what you doing? Don't be tellin' people my business."

"How do we know you can get us in?" Ron asked rather defiantly. "Don't have us come back here for nothing. We have things to do."

The younger of the brothers responded, "we can get you in because my brother can work miracles. That's all I'm gonna say."

"Hello, I'm the brother that can work miracles and have been working them for the past year and a half. I guarantee you I can get you in. I do this every night until five in the morning."

"We'd be trespassing, wouldn't we?" Ashanti asked with deep concern.

"Who's gonna tell? We're not. You only get charged with trespassing if you get caught. Every hour I take somebody through those gates. Next, I got a family of six that's going back to Australia in the morning," the younger brother affirmed.

The three huddled together to make a decision. They could always go back the following week. The young men would be an asset for tourists who could not return. But Anwar was eager. He wanted to dig right in and get any kind of help he could that would lead him to that cylinder. He would pay for Ron and Ashanti too.

"Why don't we grab a bite to eat and come back, hon?" Ron suggested.

"Good decision, my man," the younger brother said and gave them all a 'high five.'

The three were back at nine on the dot but there was no sign of the young men. Where were they? People were camping in their cars and had driven as close as they could get to the cemetery without having to pay parking fees. After looking around for fifteen minutes, one of the young men quickly approached them. He told them it would only be a ten minute walk to the unseen entrance but he lied. It was more like twenty minutes and it wasn't on the other side. It was in a dark secluded spot, dangerous. But just as they had been told, they were met by the young man's brother.

"Fifteen dollars," he said in such a low tone that his voice was barely audible.

Anwar gave the fifteen dollars to the young man and the gate was opened. He noticed that it hadn't even been locked. It appeared to have an electrical apparatus that had been deactivated. There were also light sensors that had been deactivated so they could walk around without being detected. Finally, they were in St. Louis Cemetery heading for the tomb of the greatest voodoo queen. The younger brother led the way while, the master electrician camouflaged himself with nighttime and the help of a tree ornamented in Spanish moss.

They walked as quietly as possible and were implored not to speak until they had arrived at the tomb. The ground was uneven and cracked, revealing the cemetery's age. Crickets chirped and flying things stung but surprisingly, it did not feel ghastly there. The tombs were taller than they had imagined. Some were possibly ten feet and a number of them in poor condition and more than likely were some of the oldest, dating back to the 1700's. Excitement and anticipation made the trip to the tomb long and grueling.

"This is it," the young man finally said. "Do what you have to do quietly and I'll stand watch."

Ashanti wanted to hurry out of there. She couldn't believe she was trespassing. What if something went wrong? Anwar thought the same thing. That was a behavior young people would choose. They enjoyed taking chances like that but it was too late to think that way. They were deep in the heart of the plan. The young man whispered how to carry out the ritual before he stood aside. He also told them to let him talk should they get caught.

"*Caught?*What do you mean?" Anwar demanded.

You said we can't get caught," Ashanti added, suddenly frightened by possibilities. "Didn't you tell us that?"

"Everything is possible, but it's just not probable," the young man declared.

"Man, we better not get caught," Anwar said. "You *did* assure us this was safe. We have our careers and reputations. We're all professors."

"We got this. Me and my brother got this."

They stopped talking and began rubbing and hugging the tomb, questioning themselves if they were in their right minds. Ashanti opened the bag and set liquor and cigars in front of the tomb. Anwar felt foolish and childish but fought to get that out of his mind. He had to believe! He spun around and around then tapped on the tomb with his knuckles. He whispered, "Queen Marie Laveau, I need to find Buddy Bolden's cylinders and relics. Please help me."

There appeared a sudden glow. Sadly, it had come from the flashlight of the new guard. The former guard, who had been getting a portion of the brothers' proceeds had been replaced for insubordination. This new guard would get a feather in his hat on his very first day.

"How did you get in here?" the guard growled.

"Um, the gate was opened and we just walked in," the young man stated."

"I'm traumatized. Sir, I'm pregnant," Ashanti said.

"Well, you made a decision to trespass and that's a felony. You all are gonna have to pay a fine and possibly go to jail. Alright, start walking."

They stood looking at one another, each feeling stupid and foolish. Now what? Would they go to jail? Ashanti too? Suddenly Anwar wondered who could he turn to in a city of strangers? Could he turn to Merriam? No, he could never tell her he'd been so foolish as to trespass in a cemetery to make his way to Marie Laveau's tomb. He'd done a lot of dumb things but Merriam would contend that he needed psychiatric care.

As they walked ahead of the groundskeeper, he thought about making a run for it but it was dark and he had seen the guard grasping something shiny at his side. It was a gun, no doubt. Furthermore, he would never find his way out of there and would get caught anyway. Alas, it was impasse! They all just stared in one another's faces, unable to believe what had just transpired.

At the police station, identification numbers were assigned to their mug shots which made them feel more like criminals but good natured Ron, changed their moods quickly when he reminded them that real researchers understood that trespassing went along with the territory.

"There's a detective, *a real live detective* in North Carolina that gets slapped with a trespassing violation every week. He's the top detective in the city too. This is small stuff. Researchers are detectives in their own right. I'm not worried," he said, then relaxed in the uncomfortable chair, complements of the precinct, and nodded off to sleep.

They were charged, released and given a court date. To their surprise a young journalist had followed the story. As soon as the Captain had discovered they had three professors in their custody he called the press. This would make an interesting article for the natives of New Orleans and earn the journalist, the station Captain's son, a bit of publicity. The furor he would induce was surely pending. Residents would scream, 'Who dares to come to our city and vandalize our voodoo queen's tomb? Lock 'em up and swallow the key!'

The next morning, right on the front cover of the daily newspaper, directly underneath the main headline was the mug shots of three professors and a college student. The caption read: *Three Professors and Student Caught Trespassing and Vandalizing the Tomb of Marie Laveau."*

Vandalizing? They had never done anything of the like! They were all outraged and demanded to see an official that would drop the 'vandalizing' charge.

What an embarrassment, Anwar thought. 'I just met these people and they got me in trouble already.' He thought about what his brother said about trouble finding him. 'But nobody had held a gun to my head and made me go to that cemetery,' he admitted. But he wondered if Marie Laveau would work out his requests. Time would tell but one thing for sure, going there was going to cost them. 'Come on Voodoo Queen, work some wonders now.' It seemed since his arrival in New Orleans, everything was working against him? When they were all slapped with a fifteen-hundred dollar fine and would have to pay court costs, he knew meeting the couple was not to his advantage.

It didn't take long for the news to circulate. Practically all the musicians knew what he'd done and made light fun of it. They held their newspapers up and said things like, "I am Marie Laveau" and here comes "voodoo de bassman."

Anwar would just shun them off, "aw com' on now, let's just play." But to make things worse, Merriam found out about it. Yes, Merriam. She'd been keeping up with New Orleans news. She practically jumped out of her skin when she saw Anwar's mug shot online. "What tha. . ., *what the hell is he out there doing?*"

He got a good phone lashing from Merriam.

"You're supposed to be focused on Buddy."

"I was."

"Well what were you doing at Marie Laveau's gravesite? I hope nobody in Connecticut finds out about this. I will be so embarrassed. And who were those other people?"

"Friends Merriam, just friends."

"Well you don't need friends like them!"

"Look, I didn't vandalize anything and I've got to go," he said, declining to give her anymore information. He hung up on her. How could he expect her to understand what led up to his arrest? Or understand his desperation to find Buddy's cylinder before his sabbatical would end?

The vandalizing charges were dropped the following week. That young journalist had been determined to make them examples, even to the point of lying on them. He would make it clear that no outside professors would come to Nah__'lins, not good old Nah__'lins, and think to trespass upon the grounds where their great Voodoo Queen, Marie Laveau had been resting her bones.

Anwar woke up the next morning with Stevie Wonder's song stuck in his head like a broken record, "*. . . living just enough, just enough for the city.*"

Chapter 9
Woman To Woeman

Merriam flew down to join him. She hated the weather and the bugs that wouldn't leave although it was rather cool. She complained about the people being stuck up too.

"Anwar, I saw a lady that reminded me of my mother and when I told her so, she turned up her chin. You believe that?"

"Maybe she didn't think she was old enough to look like your mother," he replied impatiently.

"Oh now? Are we taking her side?"

"You have to watch what you say to people, Merriam."

"Oh, hogwash. They're just stuck up around here."

"I haven't had much of a problem with the people."

"You wouldn't admit it if you had," she smirked and disappeared into his small kitchen.

She told him that she would probably stay the rest of her winter vacation and she did. She was very worrisome while she was there too and treated the situation as though it were a honeymoon. She wanted Anwar to do so many things with her that would take him away from his work. Whenever he refused, she complained, "see, I told you that you were going to ignore me."

"I'm being paid to do research, Merriam."

"Not to research Buddy Bolden. What if they knew?"

"I suppose you're going to go back and tell them?"

"Ha! I should. Then maybe I can get my man back!"

He had tried to avoid having any disputes with her. He hadn't had to argue with anyone in the short time he'd been there and he found himself unable to think and function properly while under the stress of a quarrel. Arguing immobilized him. 'What peace single people had that they did not realize', he thought.

Once, while they had gone shopping, Merriam bumped into a woman that had taught at her school. The two were elated to meet up. They exchanged numbers and the woman got Merriam involved in several things, from a literary club to line dance parties. This pleased Anwar and gave him freedom to get back into his work. He went at it diligently, researching everything of importance relating to Buddy.

He found no support materials to document that Buddy had been a pimp so that allegation was tossed out the window. Buddy, like many male musicians, had gotten so much admiration from women that pimping them would not have even been necessary. Women often saw to it that male performers had enough to eat, a roof over their heads and anything else they needed. Heck, a few women had been eager to take care of Anwar whenever he had encountered hard times, even Merriam. He just never took any of them up on their offers.

He tried but could not locate any of Buddy's relatives that were said to be alive. He decided to leave that alone. What he felt was equally important, however, was finding a cornet from Buddy's era that could demonstrate the kind of tone Buddy had before trumpets pushed their way into the music scene. He also researched styles of clothing Buddy might have worn, cigars and cigarettes he may have smoked, foods he may have eaten and, yes, the type of moonshine he might have drank. Every little detail he learned about Buddy seemed to empower him. Buddy had possessed his very soul. The man had only existed for a 'moment in time' but his energy was so phenomenal that it had crystallized itself into an eternal heartbeat called jazz.

Merriam had begun to unnerve him whenever she and her friend had nothing planned for the day. He couldn't stand it when she was idle.

"What's all this shit?" she asked once when Anwar covered the table with sheet music.

"Why do you have to call it shit?" he defended.

"I don't know what it is," she answered honestly.

"Precisely. So why does it have to be shit? It's my research and it's important to me. These are copies of sheet music, the earliest black jazz songs. Does that sound like shit?"

"Alright, okay! I didn't mean shit. Stuff."

"Now it's stuff. This is stuff? Merriam, just don't say anything to me for the next twenty minutes. Please?"

"I'll do better than that. I won't say anything to you for the rest of the day."

"Thank you."

" And I'll be having dinner alone tonight, Anwar."

"Yeah, sure. Whatever." He didn't protest. He needed space. And that would be his new year's present. Space.

Merriam wound up staying until the last minute. School would start the following week which meant she would have to cram hours and hours into her planning over one weekend to be ready for the children.

"Anwar, promise me you'll be good? Promise?" she begged before boarding the plane.

"Promise," he said, feeling childish again and having no idea what 'be good' had meant.

"I'm going to keep up with this city's news again. Please don't do anything to damage your career. There is life after

New Orleans, you know? And leave Marie Laveau alone."
Keep doing crazy things like that and you might get put
where Buddy went for twenty-five years."

"I won't even address that, Merriam. You have a way of
saying things that are sometimes. . . just foolish."

She tossed her chin up playfully and they kissed. Finally
she was on her way. He stood watching as the plane sped
down the runway then powerfully invaded the sky.

"Gone. Anwar gets life back," he said, as the plane
became just a dot. "Yes!" He took himself out to dinner and
downed a whole bottle of champagne. Man, did she get on
his nerves, especially when she spoke to him about
marriage.

He'd made a mistake the first week he'd arrived in New
Orleans by confessing how much he had missed her. So in
his most aching solitude, when he couldn't even play
Bassetta, he called and asked, "would you marry me, baby,
if I asked you to?"

"Are you proposing?"

"Yeah, I guess I am. Baby, I miss you. I love you."

Well, he had meant it, at least he had at the time, but the
separation helped him break his dependency to her and he
really hadn't missed her after the second week. He did love
her but he had new insight into life. He had begun to enjoy
his bachelorhood. He'd met women more talented, intelligent and attractive than her. He only looked at and talked
to them but at least the veil had been lifted. He'd always
thought Merriam was the best he could have but he'd met
women in New Orleans that he felt could put Merriam to
shame. Many of them were dedicated artists and could
address his inner well of passion. He often wondered if he
should try to find someone artistically stimulating but when
he was reminded of the many aimless relationships he'd
once had he just couldn't put his heart into starting all over
again.

Chapter 10
Wrath Of The People

New information was slowly emerging about Buddy. For instance, Buddy hadn't played a horn professionally until his early twenties. That meant he cultivated all that greatness in less than ten years. Buddy had fathered a son and a daughter and presumably had been married at least once. An old man told him Chas had been a nickname for Buddy's first name, Charles. The rumor was that the word 'jazz' came about by error. The music Buddy played was respectively labeled 'Chas' by the people. When he'd get all hot, blowing out a loud and soulful melody, people would shout, "play that Chas, play that Chas." Years later, intentionally or through human err, 'Chas' was changed to 'jazz'. But some researchers purported that 'jazz' was an offensive term whites used to label blacks improvised music. 'Jazz,' had once meant noise and clamor. There could be veracity in that research since black music was scorned heavily in those days. Another rumor claimed that Ragtime got its name not only because of its 'peculiar' timing but also because those 'blacks' that played it appeared to be 'raggedy' or wearing 'rags.' But however the names came about, jazz and ragtime had long redeemed their honor.

According to numerous researchers, Buddy played a lot of songs in B-flat and he didn't just drink huge amounts of alcohol but he drank it all day long. Whether it had been out of frustration or in an attempt to silence his intensity, he did indeed drink like a fish. 'Could Buddy's dementia have evolved from a deep depression that was aggravated by contaminated moonshine? If moonshine could suddenly destroy vision, could it also destroy the brain?'

Buddy's favorite pastime according to some books, was hanging out at his friend's barbershop. Buddy himself was said to have been a laborer which could have encompassed carpentry, plastering and even painting. But most times he made a living playing his music.

Two pictures of Buddy had surfaced. One was a portrait in oil and the other was a black and white photograph taken with his band members. The pictures did not resemble one another in the least. The photograph was the most reliable in suggesting how Buddy might have really looked. It was a little grainy but Anwar went with that. Buddy had been very good looking too. It was reported that he had so much charisma that women fought over who would carry his belongings. One woman might carry his horn, another would carry his coat, and another would carry his umbrella. Incidents like that conjured up the rumor that he had been a pimp.

The saddest aspect of Buddy's life, however, that which had made him and Beard cry, was that he had been committed to an insane asylum at twenty-nine years old. *A young man!* He never saw the inside of a club again. There he spent twenty-five years locked away until his death.

One late autumn day after heavy research, Anwar pulled to the side of the road in front of one of his favorite spots to count out a few bucks for dinner. He recognized two men as the same ones that did not want to tell him anything about Buddy. They had been watching him with frowns on their faces. He didn't think much of the sneers they had given him because he had grown accustomed to people confronting him or threatening to give him a good beat down. So the triflin', dirty looks he'd gotten meant nothing. He nodded at the men and returned their sneer, then entered the restaurant. But when he left out an eerie feeling overcame him. He looked around but saw no one. He peeped into his car and saw that his notebook was not in the location where he had left it. Several boys played softball at a distance and he wondered if maybe one of them had gone into his car searching for something worth taking. He decided he would not make a fuss about it but would remember to lock his doors in the future. But before he could climb into the car someone grabbed his left arm and yanked him, hard. It was one of the two men that had stood out front. He felt a sharp pain in his neck but he would have to ignore it and prepare to fight. Before he could make a fist the other man stepped out of hiding, grabbed his other arm and yanked him in the opposite direction. Like children playing hide and seek, the two men had hidden and waited until Anwar had left the restaurant.

"What you writin' about Buddy for? Eh? Didn't we warn you to leave things be? Every time one of yawl out of town folks come, you go away tellin' lies," said one man.

"No, I don't tell lies in my research!" Anwar defended.

"Well somebody do. We played jazz first; us blacks right here in New Orleans. But people got all kinds of folks saying they played it first. We ain't gonna read ya lies no more!" he said, with a fiery anger.

"Our black people played jazz all over this country, not just in New Orleans. Buddy was the first one to play it in America. An' they couldn't make us shame of it either," said the other man with an intensified anger.

The men were unusually angry because of what had occurred so many years ago. Anwar understood. History books had been so full of lies until the United Nations had published a magazine that would rewrite history as it had truly happened and not simply from a Eurocentric perspective or from any other view. Its' purpose was to record the truth. But *other* researchers had lied about Buddy. He hadn't. *He wouldn't.* He was on Buddy's side.

"I told you! I don't report lies!" Anwar yelled and struck out at one of the men. But the other man hit Anwar so hard that he knew his jaw had to be broken. He slowly lifted his head off the ground. He was dizzy, dumbfounded, as the men took off running. With hazy vision he pulled himself up by his van's door handle. He peered into the side view mirror and saw that his lip had been busted and a long chain of blood flowed down his shirt. He discovered his notebook wedged between the door and seat on the passenger's side. It was empty of the new notes he'd just written but they had not gotten far. They had been torn into small pieces and dumped on the back floor. He'd worked hard to collect those notes. He gathered them together and placed them back into the notebook. He walked around the car slowly, checking for scratches and dents but he didn't find any. Listlessly he wandered under a nearby tree and stared pitifully at his SUV. He saw that his dinner had been dumped on its hood. His heart was broken. A stream of tears rolled down his face, neck and then chest. Why had he been so hated by his own people? They actually attacked him. Yes, he did intend to share some of the information with whites but he did not intend to exploit Buddy's memory in the least. He was there for the proliferation of Buddy's legacy too, not just for himself, although finding Buddy's relics could enhance his life. The lip and jaw would heal quickly but his heart would ache far longer.

'What was this'?! Something was happening to him. People and pictures were in his head and they were racing in and out and standing right in front of him and speaking without moving their mouths. He saw old jazz musicians leaning on buildings. Buddy was there, Bunk Johnson was there, and other musicians. Even Marie Laveau's tomb was there. He saw the girl that had hustled him. She was there arching her fingers at him as though she were going to scratch him in the face. Merriam, Beard, Gil, and people in his old neighborhood were there. He saw the cocktail waitress at his favorite bar, old band members, Zack, an old wino and his black history professor. They all were zooming in and out in brilliant colors, fading and returning and zooming in and out again, spinning and leaping out at him and then he heard words from within and around. Who was that speaking? Who was that saying. . .

"just maybe you had presented yourself separate from the people. You walked arrogantly amongst the poor, jobless and hungry black sisters and brothers living in the most dilapidated parts of the city wearing your eleven-hundred dollar suits and five-hundred dollar shoes. These people watched you climb out of a brand new SUV while the majority of them had never even owned a car and definitely not a new one. There were the homeless watching you as you turned up your nose and wrote things in your notebook about them while kicking aside the very card-board they had used the night before as a roof. You hopped from one side of buildings to the other never wondering how and why they were decayed and abandoned and never wondered why money wasn't being pumped into the poorest sections of the city when New Orleans, French Quarters, had flourished as one of the richest tourist sites in the world. You shook your head when panhandlers asked you for money and you made sure you didn't make contact with them if you had obliged. You watched with disgust the quarreling couples with the weight of water and electric bills on their shoulders while minimum wage jobs had been their reality for the past, present and possibly future. You fanned the air and squeezed your nostrils together when

'old man Clay,' who smelled of urine told you about Buddy's relatives and about moonshine back then. Every-day you wiped the tops and bottoms of your shoes with napkins and tossed them on their streets before you entered your ride. You pursed your lips together and shook your head when you saw skillful musicians playing on corners and curbs for donations instead of appearing in upscale clubs, never realizing they'd also chosen freedom. You used to be a brotha but you forgot who you were as you climbed the ladder to success. As far as the people are concerned you are their enemy, a mocking piece of shit, earning eighty-thousand dollars in less than a year and you only wanted to spend as much time in their world as you needed, get what you wanted and then leave them with nothing. Why the hell would they want to give you any information? They'd seen Negroes like you before. You don't plan to split the book proceeds or the money you make from Buddy's cylinder with them so they can fix up their crooked porches. That book or cylinder wasn't going to come back and build a rec center for their children. It wasn't going to do a thing for them. And they would watch that book make its way across the world and make a publisher rich and famous who never even loved Buddy, less lone his people; somebody who would not even dedicate a page to Buddy's family or walk through the neighborhood to spend time just mingling and 'kicking it' with the sistahs and brothas. They would never see your face again until you wanted something else from them. Same ol' story. And Buddy's cylinder would make sure you got paid for getting your face on the cover of every jazz journal and you'd never take a dime back to the place Buddy called home. Hell no, they didn't want you around. You aren't like Buddy who gave his soul until he had none for himself. You aren't like Brother Tunde who taught young men how to read right in his own living room or like Brother Kudjo that loved the people or like Sistah Daniels who ran the SafeHood Program to educate the

youth about the dangers of drugs and how to promote unity in their neighborhoods. You aren't like Brother Cal who is the attorney for the poor and never charged the people more than a few bucks in exchange for his legal representation. You don't have a mission to help promote positive growth anywhere for anyone. You are right up there with the cops that went into their neighborhood and carried off Lottie's son and locked him up for three years because he stole two packs of meat to feed his hungry family. You are the Negro that won't hire the black boy because he doesn't own a suit, never understanding that he and his mother had to get the money up for his decent pair of shoes first. You are like the john that visited Sweet Sonya who after she was done with made sure he got knocked in the head and robbed. You are like the white suburban coke addicted businessman coming 'down the way' in a Lamborghini to 'cop' from the slums then talk about black folks to his friends and family, saying 'those people live like goddamn roaches.' You are apolitical and will present the people as decadent when Africa's stolen human cargo have been squashed by oppression for years and you are on the oppressor's side. You are scum.

The images grew less and less until they had faded away. *He thought*: The French Quarters continues to grow filthy rich from the style Buddy played. Tourists peel off their clothes and dance, and spend millions of dollars, to walk around with drinks in their hands and act like wild animals while the people Buddy loved experiences a 'slow demise. He realized he'd often lived in a fairytale, sipping large expensive margaritas at sidewalk cafés while his poor sisters and brothers passed him by perhaps thinking, 'one day, I'm gonna have a seat right there and be served.' He thought that the school children that ran home may not have had school supplies and may have shared a bedroom with five siblings. He remembered while still in Connecticut how he refused to give a crack addicted mother money to buy milk for her baby and said nothing in her defense when she was arrested for stealing a quart from a bodega. Once a homeless, schizophrenic, barefoot dreamer with a linty and dirty afro, wearing a grimy white laced dress and having crusty heels and toes, peered into his face and asked him, "sir, who are you and are you really who you say you are?" He realized that there was sanity to her madness. No, the people of New Orleans didn't need anyone like him around. *The people were panged* and still most of them had enough love to nod their heads and smile at him when he'd come around. A punch in the jaw was like a tap on the hand. That was stern comeuppance but he was lucky he hadn't caught a 'cap' in his behind.

He understood, firsthand, why Giles had to send a black man to do research but even blacks were in grave danger. Black people in New Orleans loved Buddy! They loved him immensely. They celebrated his very life while the rest of the world enjoyed the byproducts of his music and ironically some would never know the great man behind the sound of jazz that stole their souls so completely.

Like the rape of Africa, people came and took from New Orleans and never gave anything back. They distorted facts, denied the people's greatness, stole and borrowed without ever, ever giving anything back to the people who had showcased their culture and performed dances and rituals, jumping eight feet high in the middle of Congo Square with plumes, masks, cowry shells and secrets of the universe. America cursed the peoples culture—voodoo was always misunderstood, even by some blacks but it was far too mystical, cultural and complex to be judged by a western world. Yet, those persons who were honest and fair, trickled down to the black carnivals and jazz festivals and admitted their fascinations with the little piece of Africa, allowing themselves to be magically charmed by its black inhabitants.

Anwar thought about how he had even accused the so-called mulattoes for the mistreatment of darker skinned blacks when they too were products of oppression. Victims. Indoctrinated. From the time they were labeled mulattoes, quadroons, octoroons, they'd been victims from the time light-skinned black women were made to cover their nappy heads as not to be mistaken for white women, they'd been victims; from the time the door of no return swallowed up black Africans who were then dispersed in foreign lands, they'd been victims. From the time jazz bubbled out of the cotton fields until the time Buddy had violently blown it out of his horn, blacks had been victims and the victims of Naw__'Lins on that day, had had enough.

He felt sick, as if he needed to spit up or just take in a lot of air. His car sat glistening quietly like a get away coach. After a few deep breaths he made a slow and painful twist to get behind the wheel. When he'd driven a few miles he spotted a small courtyard and jumped out of the car to think. Several couples were walking and holding hands. He walked too, trembling all the while as he thought fiercely about Buddy's life. 'Oh, how Buddy must have sat by the roadside with his head down because nobody wanted to believe that a young black musician could create such depth. 'Nigger music, jungle bushman music they had called it. Yes! Damn right, it was jungle! Yes, it was bushman. Right out of Africa! And it was honestly conceived. It had been essentially a memory from where his weary soul had traveled.' It was a music that reached his core. American music did not do that for him, so in an attempt to unite with his true sound, the black jungle boy created a revolution. He didn't intend to do so. He'd simply desired to vibe on a music of his own understanding.

How Buddy must have drank and staggered from the clubs he 'hit at.' Lord! The world must not have meant a thing to him when he picked up his horn. How his mother must have melted when the papers reported that her baby, her fucking baby boy had clobbered his mother-in-law. But his mother was not swayed by the whispers. It had not been Buddy that had struck the woman. It had been the ghost of sadness that lingered in the shadows of his existence.

His mother understood her child was a genius and that everybody hates a genius. And when her baby cried out 'Mama, the music in my head, it plays on and on and on', she knew his well ran too deep. How she must have crumbled when her baby took that long ride to the insane asylum in a wretched crowded wagon pulled by a team of dusty horses. And when he finally bowed out of the sorry ass world of bloodsuckers, murderers, liars and thieves to spend twenty five years talking to himself and picking things off the wall that were not there, she might have felt that he had been in better hands tucked away like that than be stabbed over and over in the truth of his existence until he had succumbed from his very gist. Oh God, Buddy!'

Anwar was weak. He sat on the ground by a tree not giving a damn about the grass stains on his four-hundred dollar slacks or the blood on his six-hundred and forty dollar jacket. He was so absorbed in the hull of Buddy that he did not know he was crying. But he knew that he would have to leave Buddy alone! The musical genius of New Orleans was tearing him apart, literally destroying him.

But he thought he heard a whisper. It may have been just the faint rustle of leaves or the far away shriek of a child's cry. It said, *'Tell them'*. Suddenly Buddy stood beside him and breathed out, 'Chas'. Then it clicked. After all the years of obsession over the man that called his chil'ren home, he finally knew why he was there. Fate did not send him to research Giles' marching bands but Buddy had 'called him' and had rested uneasily in his ancestral chamber until he had shown up. He realized that Buddy had chosen him when he was a skinny kid just as much as he had chosen Buddy. And there stood Buddy's ghost begging for acknowledgement. That had been the very thing he lacked, that which had sent him away to melt inside those asylum walls. He hadn't needed a lot of money from the dance halls or a roomful of women to admire his good looks. Those things could never validate his musicianship. He simply needed respect and the proper acknowledgement of his great contribution which had been severely violated. It had been left up to Anwar to set free the ghost of Buddy, which had haunted him from the day he and Beard had cried together. The ghost must return across the waters, to his plumes and drums and cowry shells, where he could rest his weary soul.

Anwar rose to his feet, wholly renewed. He looked around boldly and shouted in his loudest voice, "I'LL TELL THEM. I'LL TELL THEM FOR YOU, MAN! Then he yelled out "BUDDY," for a full five seconds.

People looked at him. The ladies were fearful and backed up to their men who embraced them tightly. The children ran to their mothers and pointed at his bloody clothes, and people who had been in cars shook their heads and pressed their locks. Feeling fatuous and ashamed, he ran to his car, jumped inside and 'peeled rubber,' sending pedestrians scattering and running for their lives.

He told Merriam about the incident that night. She tried to decipher the vision but wound up doubting his sanity instead. Maybe he just felt guilty about going to Marie Laveau's grave. Maybe everything was over a guilty conscience. . . Yeah, that's the way it had appeared.

Merriam screamed and hollered on the phone as though someone had been attacking her. "Baby, come home. Please! Two things our people don't trust is a white man and a black man snooping around for a white man. I knew you shouldn't have taken that job!"

"Merriam, Merriam, calm down. I'm not coming home. This was the first time anything like this has ever happened to me. Wait! Listen! Won't you just calm down? Please!" He might as well have been talking to himself. In fact, he discovered he had been talking to himself. Merriam had hung up.

CHAPTER 11
OH OH!

Anwar's jaw had still not healed and it was already over three weeks since the incident. It appeared crooked and swollen and he was having difficulty chewing. He went to see a doctor who referred him to a bone specialist. He ordered x-rays and consulted with another specialist before breaking the news to him.

"You have scar tissue growing partially over the socket where the joints fit together. You're going to need surgery to remove it before we can reset your jaw."

"It's that bad?"

"Yes it is," said the black specialist who was so down to earth that Anwar was compelled to say 'what's up brotha?'

"If you'd come to us right away we could have reset it but now you need surgery. You don't have to get it done immediately," Dr. Knox explained, "but you'll continue having difficulty chewing until you do. If you wait too long you might start having pain because the scar tissue is covering up a large portion of the joint and that may began pushing your jaw further out of alignment. Dr. Bhargava will perform the surgery with me."

With a heavy accident, Dr. Bhargava said, "cordect, and it should only take a few howas. We will place peens in your jaw and wire it almost shut for the 'eeling to take place. Aftah a while we weel remoove dee peens and you be ghould to go. But you weel not bee abo to opeen your mout wide and you weel 'ave to juse and bleend your food and dreenk from a straw until we remoove dee peens."

"Oh no, no. I can't do that. I'm here working on an assignment. Can't this wait until I get back home?"

"It can wait but should be done within a year or you will have some serious trouble," Dr. Knox, warned. "And there's no guarantee you won't need more surgery when you do decide to get it done. And please, don't get hit in that jaw again or you may have a permanent deformity."

"I won't. And I'll get it done when I get back home."

"That's fine, as long as it gets done," Doctor Knox warned. "That kind of injury is nothing to play with."

In the weeks to follow, Anwar dedicated all of his time to researching Buddy. He only broke for a cigarette, to eat, to wash his behind, and make love to Bassetta, in the form of jazz. And when he went among the people, he was an entirely different Anwar. He had started dressing mostly in jeans and t-shirts too and he was as respectful as possible when dealing with everyone. He offered the homeless a meal. He took a few suits to an employment program for young men who were looking for work. He gave donations to youth organizations and he even gave a donation to a music school to help buy instruments. Giving made his research more enjoyable but he vowed he would not get caught up with people again unless it was absolutely necessary.

He felt a little lonely but didn't have time to socialize. Plus his last episodes, the twins, then Ron and Ashanti made him leery of people. No. No more people in his life. Just his work. People were damning. He did break down and contact Ron and Ashanti by phone but resolved himself to be one of their distant friends. Telephone contact would be more than enough. Besides, he knew about deadlines and they had a habit of sneaking upon you. The further he stayed ahead of them the better off he would be. But he was gregarious sometimes. He loved deep, meaningful conversation and a little party now and then. But no, only tunnel vision would be conducive to getting results. It was time for him to get even more serious, about everything. That homeless woman's vision and her words stayed with him constantly. 'Who are you? Are you really who you say you are'? So piercing. That made him work so consistently that his eyes burned and watered all the time. But that was okay. He didn't really want a break. He had wasted enough time messing around in the clubs, way too much time; and messing with people. He'd also taken out time to let his jaw heal. Still he was lonely but too bad for him. Buddy came before anything else. He was playing catch up and relentlessly focused. However, sometimes. . . , even when one has tunnel vision, some ill fated thing can manifest itself. He put the desire to socialize out there—you know, into the universe and soon it was answered. Well, sort of. His mother had always warned him, "you must be careful for what you ask."

'A*las*, no man is an island.'

That Spring, Anwar's wild oats sent him seeking company. He wanted to see Merriam but she had been so busy working with a children's program that they wouldn't have been able to get together for another month. He could understand that and he would wait but he did not see any harm in entertaining female company as long as he'd kept his fly closed. His opportunity came when he played a few weeks in a trio for a jazz vocalist named Stanza. He had not been able to take his eyes off the stunning woman from the moment she stepped onto the stage to rehearse with the band. He had been expecting a full bodied, heavy bosomed blues belter to join them, about 55 years old. She'd have a sixty year old boyfriend who'd sit at the reserved table directly in front of the stage and nibble on toothpicks. His chest would be puffed up so large until everyone in the audience would know he was her fellow. Anwar was wrong though. Curved and vivacious this woman was, outdoing Merriam. She owned a waistline that must have been about 18 inches. Her legs were meaty and shapely and she drove Anwar wild when she crossed them. As if that wasn't enough, she was a mesmerizing vocalist, close to Ella in scatting and Sarah in range. She was a deep satiny brown color and wore ruby red lipstick. She had long jet black dreadlocks that she curled and put into wild hairstyles that often covered one eye. When she would wiggle during a number in her fancy body-fitting dresses, Anwar couldn't concentrate. He wanted to be out in the audience getting a full view of this gorgeously, talented woman. But he had learned his lesson quite well about dating women he worked with so he waited until his two weeks stint in her band was up then asked her out. She obliged and they went to an after hours club, which was known back in the day as a speakeasy or juke joint.

Stanza was one of the most fascinating women he'd ever met. She had been a legal secretary but quit her job after her debut on a local television program in Michigan. She selected awesome musicians and traveled all over the world performing. She'd spent three years in Paris, a year in Japan and a year in Africa. She cried when she heard Billie and felt sassy when she listened to Sarah. Like Anwar she worked all the time perfecting her craft. He told her about Merriam and his assignment in New Orleans and about Marie Laveau and his fifteen-hundred dollar trespassing fine. She found it hilarious. He also told her why his jaw looked a little crooked too.

"Your jaw doesn't look crooked to me. Where's it crooked?" she asked, tilting her head to get a different perspective. "Hmmm, it still looks normal to me. If it's crooked it's just not noticeable."

"Not to you. And that's because you just met me. People who already know me would see that it's crooked."

"If you say so," she said nonchalantly. "You're still handsome."

He instantly felt himself falling for Stanza, but quickly caught himself. Quickly. Besides she had not had time for a boyfriend in three years and had been celibate since that last one. Still, his adulation for her could not be contained.

"I'm going to tell you the truth, Anwar. Men want to possess me. They see me, think I'm beautiful and just like a flower they want to pluck me up and take me home. The problem is that they have taken me from the source I draw from and I die. Literally. My life comes apart. So I just stay alone. I need all my energy for me and I have never found a man that I can be with that doesn't absorb my energy."

Anwar assured her that he understood and would not follow in the path of the others. In turn, she felt comfortable enough for them to have a wonderful, mentally stimulating relationship and when he told her about his real mission in New Orleans she began to share his passion for Buddy. She would sometimes find information from jazz books about Buddy that Anwar had not yet discovered. It wasn't very significant information but was a new tidbit just the same and it felt good to have her on his team.

One night after having wearily climbed into bed from a long day of research, his bell was rang over and over again. He opened the door to discover Stanza. She was trembling and crying and was just a bundle of nerves. He quickly put on the tea kettle then wrapped her in blankets before he questioned her condition.

"I'm scared," she told him. "I'm really scared and don't know why. I think sometimes I'm possessed and the 'real me' is going to be consumed like what happened to Billie. You know, Billie consumed herself, not the drugs. You know that, don't you? I can't even relate to people anymore. I work all the time Anwar, all the time. And I never get tired of it. That's abnormal."

"No, that's normal for an artist. I do it too."

"But I'm so withdrawn. Even you have a life. You do other things besides work. You go bike riding."

"No. I *went* bike riding with a sightseeing tour group but only once--and when I first came to New Orleans."

"Well, I never have. I just sing. I don't even go to the grocery store anymore. My singing is the only thing that breathes for me. It's like a drug. I don't even eat. Look how skinny I'm getting. I barely call my mother anymore because I'm too busy thinking of the next song I'm going to sing and where. That's really bad isn't it? She brought me into this world and I don't take time out to call. The only reason I see you is because you're into music too. Music is all I live for. I'm never going to have a husband or children. I just know it. I don't even know how to relate to men anymore." She cried harder.

"Stanza, you have to just discipline your artistic energy. Next time you can't stop singing, turn on a radio station that plays songs you don't know."

"Then I'll scat to the music."

"Then go outside and stand in the middle of the square."

"I've done that and the square reminds me of when I used to busk. I open up and sing and people just think it's a part of the New Orleans scene and tip me. I'm telling you I'm just not human anymore. I'm, I'm a machine, maybe?"

She stopped crying abruptly then gently stroked Anwar's face. "I need to be touched Anwar. I've felt this way before and I just need to feel human again."

He pulled Stanza to her feet and began to touch her. He touched her beautiful face, long neck, arms, and thighs, her buttocks. Then he carried her to his bed and massaged her from head to toe like he did Merriam. That night he made love to Stanza. It had been wholly satisfying for the both of them for they had worked themselves into tight knots.

But he began to carry a tremendous load of guilt in the days to follow. He imagined Merriam's face, saddened and slumped over his picture at the kitchen table. But why should he feel guilty? He was still a bachelor. He could have as many women as he wanted, couldn't he?

When he saw Stanza again she was a different person. "You know what I did?" she boasted. "I went to the movies and I didn't scat to the score. Aren't you proud of me? I'm proud of me!"

They slept with one another several more times and each time she became more and more in touch with life again. She even took an interest in buying new clothes.

She called him one day, "Anwar, you have to come over here. Now! Come now!"

He hung up the phone and rushed over to her house and she led him to her closet.

"Look at all the clothes I bought and they're not for the stage! I think I'm cured. Thank you, so much."

He looked into her face which was gleaming with pride. Her eyes sparkled and she couldn't have appeared any more beautiful to him than at that moment. He kissed her right in the closet then made love to her. He went home with guilt.

She hit it off with a new neighbor in her building and they went grocery shopping together and to parties and she did not sing at any events unless she was asked. Her life had become manageable. But Anwar's life was a wreck. He felt very guilty about being with Stanza and could not shake the feeling. But he couldn't resist her and didn't want to.

She was the narcotic he'd never tried and she was lethal. She was never sexually inhibited and walked through the house stark naked turning him on again and again.

He began looking forward to their sexual rendezvous', growing hungrier and hungrier for her body, mind and soul that had become a hopeless addiction. He had also developed very strong feelings for her and thought about her more than he did Merriam. Admittedly, he had fallen in love with her and while they shared similar musical backgrounds and she had an intriguing lure that invited him inside her world, she seemed ungraspable, as if she were looking for something far beyond him. But what if he could have Stanza as his New Orleans girl and Merriam as his Connecticut girl? Her soul was much more evolved than Merriam's and she wouldn't mind sharing a man. But did she want a relationship or just touching? What power had this creature called 'woman' to make his mind bounce right off of Buddy and onto her? He did not like what was happening, yet, he couldn't shake it. This was an attraction that was more like a spell. Was it voodoo? He was hit!

Love is a splendid thing but it had not been that for Merriam. She was falling apart. Her world had been perfunctory on all levels. She was still working, but barely there, emotionally. She missed Anwar but had fought the feeling so hard until it internalized and caused a festering of nervousness, skin twitching, and an array of emotions. She would be the last to admit that she wanted to see him so desperately because it was he that created the separation in the first place. She understood his passion to research Buddy 'but it was just how he did it, how he left. It was so tacky. He could have told her he was going and she would have gotten a job there teaching but he didn't even give her a hint. That was selfish,' she often mumbled. 'Now here I am alone. I must have meant absolutely nothing to him. How do you just take off and leave someone you've been with for four years? How is it you won't tell them things'?

Some women just know when they have lost their men. She knew she and Anwar were a done deal within her soul. She felt like she'd lost him forever too. He'd been acting so mysterious, like hanging up the phone quickly after she had called and she thought she heard a woman singing in the background a few times but it may have been the stereo. But she was sure that something or somebody had captured his attention. She wasn't going to fight to win him back though. She'd given up a lot to stay in a relationship with Anwar. He had been high maintenance for a long time and the relationship was ending after all. And maybe that was a good thing because the janitress was exhausted and never found the courage to let things go. Well, somebody had called it quits for her. He had. And he did that without tact too. He hadn't said one word.

Stanza invited Anwar to her next gig. They talked after her first set. She was bubbly and attentive and he used those few moments to pour out his feelings. He finally got around to asking her to be his woman. She became quiet, almost saddened.

"Anwar, I can't commit to you that way. I just wanted you to be my friend and make love to me and help me feel my humanism again. Maybe one day I will commit to a man but not anytime soon. I told you that when we first met. I'm way too free to be in a relationship right now."

"But you said you could be with a man and let him be free and still maintain your freedom at the same time."

"Yes, I did because I don't believe in possessing or controlling a human being but I didn't say that I wanted to be in a relationship. I'm a bird, you're a bird too. Oh Anwar, you got the wrong message from me. We fly. You know how we artists are. But we all have to connect to the world now and then and that's all I needed to do. I needed to come up for air."

That angered Anwar. It was as good as telling him that he had not meant any more to her than a hard penis. He wanted her right then and there, not someday. He slammed his glass on the table and turned away. Stanza ignored his temper tantrum and rose to perform the second set.

'What did I expect to achieve by spilling my feelings out to her anyway? Commitment? From a weirdo? A showgirl? My mother would have warned me about her. She would have.' But he didn't really want her. Oh, who was he fooling? She was his dream girl, beautiful and talented, the one that could travel and perform with him. They could share interests, enjoy life together, grow old together. She filled him with pride whenever they were out. Her looks put practically every woman's to absolute shame, even Merriam's. And she could sing! But Stanza just was not feeling it.

He felt like a fool. He remained affixed to his chair, sipping his drink and comforting his diffused ego as she took the stage. "Oh well, your loss, sister," he said softly. "Anyway, I already have a woman."

She opened the next set with a song dedicated to Anwar. She sang 'My Buddy.' He was familiar with that song. It was sad, a celebration and farewell song. She sang it beautifully but the song was more like a waltz instead of jazz. He wondered, 'had he only been someone to bring her back from the dead? Had he been used?' Now she had gone and dedicated some ambiguous song to him and he didn't quite know how to take it. It was like she was preparing him for the end of their relationship. Was she telling him beforehand what she would say when he would start missing her? Or was she saying that that was what Buddy would say to him if he took his mind off of his research? Off of his music? Then again could she be saying that you'll always just be my Buddy, never my man?' "Well fuck her and her games! Just fuck her," he mumbled loud enough for patrons to hear. He left out right after the song.

The next few weeks were very healing. He watched videos of standup comedians and laughed his pain away. By the second week he was ready to resume his research. But he had wasted more time. The deadline was closer.

Chapter 12
Change Overdue

Merriam was succumbing to those womanly feelings; the kinds of feelings that made a woman draw so close to a man when lying beside him that she would like to just plant herself inside of his body. She was feeling that kind of way. And when her menstrual cycle came she was as detached from her world as could be. She even gained the concern of her family and friends. She did strange things the first day of her cycles like climbing into her car and heading towards the school until she realized three quarters of the way that it was Saturday morning and she did not work on weekends. She drank lots of wine during that time too, feeling heavy and messy and hot and miserable as her emotions visited her chest and anxiety pounded out Anwar's name. The only consolation she seemed to have had and the only people she wanted to be around was her little nephew and her fourth graders. As a matter of fact, her nephew could take the credit for giving her a newfound love for the growing things like flowers, plants, trees, moss on rocks and berries. She loved to see the glow in his eyes when she'd taught him something new about the earth and she loved how tightly and tenderly he held her in his heart. Grownups had forgotten that skill and either they squeezed a person too tightly and tenderly or not enough. Their love was careless.

But a child could love you just right, leaving no room for distrust, fear, worry and doubt . . . just love. And this relationship, Merriam and child, began to help her forget about Anwar in spurts throughout the day. But when she returned the child to her sister, Anwar stepped back into her head like thunder stomping on the sky.

She realized that she'd never been in an intimate relationship with anyone as long as she had with Anwar and his absence was haunting and as far as she was concerned, he did not deserve to be sitting upon a throne perched in the back of her mind all the time but he was and it didn't matter if she was at a meeting, in front of the classroom or even trying to grade papers, there he was, Anwar Rasual, perched upon a gaudy throne, occupying the sacrosanct space in her head with a simple grin on his face. Her brain was *her* sanctuary, yet, she could see him vividly, right there, ignoring all trespassing signs. He had started this war of absence and loneliness and he was winning. She was the one that all too often broke down and called him. She would take deep whiffs of his scent that had been left in his jackets. She was the one who just sat in that hideous armchair at his house in quietude, just sitting and sighing. What had this man done to her? Yes, they'd spent time together since he'd left but it wasn't enough and it didn't count because his mind was on Buddy, not her. She respected his research but she could no longer afford to invest her feelings in such an unappreciative and insensitive creature as Anwar. There were other creatures of the male species besides him. Many had expressed a long time interest in her.

"I can't keep my mind tied up on a fool," she'd told herself over and over aloud. The only thing that might end her duress over this wild and wonderful man was to change her life, plot her future and leave him in the past. She would make those changes right away.

She spent one whole Saturday updating her wardrobe and pumping herself up about looking good and being good to herself. At a small exclusive shop she held notorious black dresses to her body. They were stretchy fits, lacey and strapless, satiny . . . eye catching. Every woman needed that infamous black dress in her closet she'd been told.

"Would you like to try those on?"

"Oh–I, I guess I would. Do you think these are too young for me?"

"Young? Are you kidding," replied a sharply dressed saleswoman, wearing a close cut natural. "My mother shops here and let me tell you, she flaunts everything. I mean EVERYTHING! And my mother is prematurely gray. Her hair is almost white. You gotta get with it, girl. You don't look no older than twenty-five."

"Thanks, but I'm older than that."

"Not that much older than me, I bet. I'm nineteen. Hold on to this."

She placed a small flat, square piece of wood in Merriam's hand with #3 on it, indicating she would be taking three outfits into the fitting room. "Follow me."

Merriam followed the young attractive woman whose youth and the ability to strut in six inch hills like they were house slippers made her feel even more foolish to be shopping for high fashion clothing.

"Oh, here's an empty room. Now would you just look at this? Somebody just left the clothes sprawled right on the darn bench. Triflin.' Why do people do this? All they had to do was bring the clothes upfront. Our clothes are not cheap. And we're supposed to be an upscale store. You wouldn't know it by the way they leave these dressing rooms."

The young woman fussed as Merriam stood aside and waited for her to remove the outfits. After she had tidied up the small room she whispered to Merriam, *"Those clothes will have to go on the clearance rack next week.* Come back if you're interested. Okay, call me when you get a dress on. I'll be right over there," she said pointing to the opposite end of the store.

The artwork on the young lady's nails were eye-catching. Merriam had never been into her own nails like that and just wondered if she should try but first things first and owning a black dress was definitely at the top of the list.

As she tried on the first dress she could hear a few of the salesgirls talking about men and singing to the music flowing through the speaker system. She imagined them dancing and snapping their fingers and nibbling on mixed nuts that would be tucked on a shelf behind the counter. They were having themselves an exquisite time, making their jobs more endurable. Could she do that anymore? No, she couldn't. She was a teacher and she had an image to uphold. But there were a lot of teachers that 'let it all hang out,' right at the teachers meetings. "I should get loose," she said to herself softly. "I should go right out there when I'm done and join them and dance in the aisles and talk about men too."

The mirror was 'bad mouthing' Merriam as it told her she was gaining weight in the wrong places. She realized ever since Anwar had left she'd taken little interest in her appearance and had been overeating for consolation. She devoured foods she'd never touched before. A diet was on the agenda if she didn't want to lose her figure. She had taken pride in her small waistline and full hips that kept men whistling and flirting with her. She needed those attributes more than ever for the new life she'd soon have.

She stuck her head out of the dressing room and the young lady quickly strutted in her direction.

"This one is a little tight. I have gained weight. I've always been able to wear a size 8."

"You should work out."

"I would but I don't have time."

"Lemme see."

The young lady tugged on the black lace dress. "I love this dress. It looks okay on you."

"But my clothes always fit better than this. I'm so mad at myself for gaining this weight."

"I'm telling you, you should go to the gym. This dress will be loose on you in no time. I go to an aerobics class three times a week. My sister just had a baby and she has already burned that weight off. There are some handsome men there too, she cooed. Single men. We all go bowling after our Tuesday class and have so much fun and girl, my mother be right there with us. I'm tellin' ya, my mother is something else! You tell her she's almost fifty and you might get cussed out. Well, you want this dress?"

"I don't know yet. Let me try on the other ones."

As Merriam slipped on the next dress she thought about the aerobics class. That would definitely be something she could benefit from. Plus she would be able to meet new people, men and women. She couldn't remember the last time she had gone out with the girls for drinks. Anwar had been her whole life for the past few years and she never wanted that to happen again.

Ahhhh, yes. She loved the fit of the second dress. She stuck her head out of the door and the young lady appeared instantaneously.

"Where's this gym?" Merriam asked without giving the young lady a chance to get inside the dressing room.

"On Shandow Road. You can't miss it. There's a huge boxing glove on the building."

"Oh, I've seen that building. I know exactly where it is."

"That boxing glove needs to come down. They say the boxing ring in that place has been closed for ten years. Now that one looks really good on you. I wouldn't lie. That is you."

"I think so. I like this one."

"You got bottom curves like my sister," the young lady added. "One day I'm gonna grow me an ass. Least that's what my mother and aunts say. I wish that day was here already. I got the smallest ass in my family. But I'm the smartest one in my family. I was offered four full scholarships. I'm in college now and I get straight A's.

"Alright now," Merriam shrieked. "Toot that whistle. Butts don't get scholarships, brains do."

They laughed and made small talk while Merriam tried on the third dress. She decided to take the second and third one.

"That'll be five-hundred and thirty dollars plus tax."

"Okay."

"Cash or credit?"

"Credit."

Merriam extended her credit card and walked away with two lovely black dresses that would be sure to turn heads.

"Oh, by the way, my name is Syra," said the saleswoman. I work here three hours a day, four days a week.

"I'm Merriam."

"Well, nice to meet you, Merriam. You try to make it to the gym now," the young lady begged.

"I will. I promise."

Merriam made it to the gym the following week. The first session proved to be highly exhilarating. She showered and got dressed quickly and headed to the reception desk.

"How can I help you?" the fitness attendant asked while sipping on a green smoothie.

"I'd like to buy a six month membership," Merriam answered, proudly.

"Wonderful, my sister. You won't be sorry." Your health is your wealth.

Chapter 13
In Healing Hands

The Thursday teacher's meeting was sure to be as they had always been; laboriously long, never really tackling the agenda but just sweeping over it lightly and never following up to bring solutions to the table. But don't show up and the Principal's wrath would be the other option.

There was a new teacher at the meeting, a man. He was teaching fifth grade. One good stare and anyone could see that he couldn't rate with Anwar's good looks. He was very regular, body and all-but he did have something that Anwar may not have had as much of: *a brain*. He was brilliant as he interjected his thoughts into the room of mostly women teachers who couldn't take their eyes off of him. Merriam concluded that there was something extremely attractive about an intelligent man. Now Anwar was no slouch in the brain department but he wasn't as sharp as this man. As the man drove point after point across to the attendees she noticed he'd cut his eyes over at her several times but maybe she was just imagining it but as soon as the meeting was adjourned he made his way toward her while several teachers made their way toward him. They shook his hand and thanked him for his ingenious input but his attention was obviously on Merriam. He tried to cut his conversations as short as he could with the others but some of the women teachers were very talkative. Some were even flirtatious.

"I'm so sorry, but can you give me a minute," he said to Merriam.

She looked around in disbelief. 'Is he talking to me? Give him a minute for what? I have to get home', she said to herself but at the same time enjoyed the butterflies his voice had awakened inside her belly. She hadn't reserved much time in her life for adults since Anwar had left. She didn't have patience for them anymore and she had little trust in them. She loved the 'honest bones,' the kids. Besides, she had promised her little nephew they would go see the ducks at the pond. She had checked out a few books about ducks from the school library to read to him when they'd gotten there. But this new teacher wanted to talk to her about something. 'What? What did this man want?'

She stood off to the side waiting patiently. After about five minutes he made his way over to her.

"I'm sorry. I guess being new warrants all that," he grinned. "Listen, I think I know you. Did your people ever live on Overlook Way?"

Merriam pulled back and a puzzled frown ran across her face. "Overlook Way? Yes. We lived on that street for years."

"Well, remember the Hamiltons?"

"I remember the Hamiltons. I sure do. I remember Stephanie and Oleta."

"Those are my sisters. I have a brother named Darrell. I'm the baby, Randy."

"Oh, my goodness! I remember you. We walked home from school together with Kathy and Omar all the time. They lived on Sackmore Street."

"Yep, yep. It's been years! How have you been?" He grinned brightly at Merriam, flashing his beautiful teeth.

"I've been fine."

"You sure look fine. I had a crush on you back then."

"Oh stop it."

"No, I did. Um, are you in a hurry?"

"Well sort of. Why?"

"I was going to offer you a sandwich and a cup of coffee."

Merriam checked her watch. "Well, I can take about an hour I guess. I have to pick up my little nephew and you can never disappoint kids."

"Hey, don't I know. I have a daughter myself. I'm a single father. My ex-wife—well, she's just not in the picture anymore. But it's all good. You ever been to Pudgy's?"

"Oh, I love Pudgy's. I try to stay away though because that name implies something I don't want."

"Heh heh, you mean you don't wanna be pudgy? Aw shucks." They both laughed.

Merriam loved his personality and she found him comfortable to be around. For the first time in a long time she relaxed.

Before the hour was up she learned his ex-wife was a doctor and traveled a lot, too much to be a good wife and mother, she told him. So they filed for divorce and he was awarded custody of their daughter when she was only thirteen months old while his wife was granted visitation rights. Merriam talked about Anwar a little and was convinced to go on a real date with Randy and she knew exactly what she would wear when that time came. The problem would be deciding which black dress it would be.

By the end of the week they'd met again. It was casual. She drove to his house to meet his little daughter as he had requested of her. His daughter was a bubbly four year old and if Merriam had ever met such a darling child who was cute and bright, this little girl was it. Of course, she wouldn't trade her nephew for the world but this child was rare and she had the cutest natural hairstyle with a little bow burrowed into it. She would love to have this child accompany her and her nephew on their little escapades. After ten minutes of talking and holding dolls, Merriam said goodbye to the little girl, her sitter, who was her great-aunt, and she and Randy rode off. This time they went to a diner that had a live band. Merriam could not stop staring at Randy. There was this, this something about him that was innocent and so real, so honest. Anwar lacked those qualities, especially innocence. He'd done practically everything under the sun; well not really but he'd been around and around the block and hadn't taken off his running shoes. But he was trying and had come a long way. But with this honest and trusting man, she could breathe. This is when she had a 'tell all' moment. Under a blaring candle with a burnt orange glow, Merriam sadly confessed her concerns and told a few secrets.

"I do love Anwar but he doesn't want marriage or children."

"What do you want?"

"The opposite of what he wants, I guess."

"Let me ask you this—why are you still with this jerk?"

"Well Anwar has his good points. You have to know him to see that he's really a very good person."

"He tells his girl of two years that he doesn't want the baby he helped her make and you abort it and then keep seeing him because he has a few good points? No, baby, you don't deserve that. You deserve a home and a family or whatever else you want."

"I know."

"Then don't let him do that to you. You know what? When he comes back and acts like an ass hole, I'll be there for you. I would like to get married again. I would like to have more children too. Tell him that. I bet he'll get his act together then. I tell you, I don't understand these guys. They get a good woman like you and treat them like they're some old common thing. You're not common and you're not a doormat. Look, I'm sorry but brothers like that just burns me up."

Merriam lowered her head thinking 'Anwar wasn't all that bad. He was a little selfish and hotheaded but that could be fixed. Or could it be'?

Randy spun around on his stool to think into the air for a second or two. "You only live once, baby" he said. He paid the tab while she sat quietly, just thinking. "You 'bout ready?"

"I am if you are. Oh, I'm so stuffed. I'll have to do two hours at the gym tomorrow." They left the diner laughing.

After about a week or so Randy called again. He was frantic. "Hey, listen, I know this is short notice but I could really use some assistance. I have these kids, you know. About thirty. I'm taking them to see The Wiz at the downtown theatre."

"What? On a Saturday morning? Did you volunteer for this?"

"No, no no. They're students from my last two schools. A lot of them are a little difficult and I'm trying to like, change their lives. One positive experience can put a kid on a better path. I bought these tickets about two months ago and the brother that was supposed to help me with the kids backed out. Baby, I need help or I'm gonna wind up losing a thousand dollars on those tickets. I know that's not a lot of money but I really want to see those kids enjoying that play but I can't handle them alone. When I say they're difficult, they are. Can you help a brother out? Now if you already have plans I could get my sister to do it but she hasn't changed much since we were kids. She's gonna fuss."

Merriam heard him talking but was thinking of his selflessness and dedication. "You spent your own money to give those kids a chance? That is so honorable! Of course I'll help. What time does the show start? And how will we get there?"

"Three o'clock. A friend of mine will drive us there in his bus. I got eighteen girls from eleven to fifteen and twelve boys from ten to fourteen. You take the girls, I'll take the boys?"

"It sounds like an adventure and I love adventures," Merriam replied with a yawn.

"You don't know what this means to me! I'll be there to pick you up at about twelve."

"I'll be ready."

The play had been superb. The children were very well behaved except for a small fight between two girls and of course they had been fighting over a boy. But the best thing about the trip is that the children had sang songs they'd heard in the play and were interested in theatre from set designing to acting.

The bus was loud and the trip was bumpy but finally the children were gone. They'd all been dropped off at their doorsteps and Randy walked Merriam to hers.

"I'm drained," he confessed.

"Oh, you let a few little children get you down? Softee," Merriam said with a giggle.

"We have to get together again. Just me and you this time. I know we talked about it but let's make it happen. You're a lot of fun, lady, you know that? What are you doing next weekend?"

Merriam looked in the air and tilted her head back and forth for nearly thirty seconds, "uuuuummmmmmmm, nothing."

"Ha! You're a silly lady. Well, you are doing something and it's with me. I got a real nice little place in mind. *Or* are you worried about that, what's his face?"

"Anwar?"

"Yeah, him."

"Last time I checked, I lived alone."

"Awwww, don't give me that crap." He laughed loudly. "I know how you ladies are. You say you're independent and done with the guy and while you're on a date you're looking around to see if he's in the room."

"Well, you don't know me. I'm not like that."

"Yeah, we'll see. I'll give you a call next Friday. Bring some dancing shoes."

"Oh, it's gonna be one of those nights?"

"You better believe it."

Ambitiously garnering Merriam's affections, a slow wet kiss was the weapon he drew to try and break Anwar's grip on the beautiful woman. She was reluctant to receive it but recognized that old familiar feeling in her pelvis that Anwar catapulted with his elaborate embraces. But this was another man. How dare she! Yes, how dare she put aside her thoughts of Anwar and kiss him back, *longingly*, basking in his newness. 'Anwar just didn't know. He could be second fiddle or on his way out', she thought.

"You know this has been a fantasy of mine's ever since we were kids, you and me? I better stop before you think I'm corny," Randy said gearing up for another kiss.

"You're corny using the word, corny" she said with a soft smile.

He kissed her again, grabbing the back of her neck and pulling her body closer to his this time. She kissed him back as though he were Anwar. When he pulled her even closer she felt others things. Sparks, quivers, and things that could lead to moans and touching and very intimate games. She just couldn't let herself go that way. It was too soon. She backed away as if she'd done something wrong. Fumbling in her small purse, she removed a large set of keys.

"I'm, I'm sorry," Randy whispered. "I'm gonna give you space. I'm gonna give you time. I promise. But that brother better not mess up. You tell him that for me. Tell him there's a man that thinks you're everything and he's waiting to make you happy and secure and shower you with some real true love."

"Stop talking like that. And just for your information, I won't be going to bed with anyone. I don't cheat and I don't pleasure myself just for the thrill of it. Sex has purpose in my life. I just wanted to let you know that."

"I didn't ask you to go to bed with me."

"Your kiss did. Yep, it said it loud and clear."

"Oh? And you think yours didn't?"

He let out a playful yelp and walked to the bus in long strides.

This man was wonderful! But a heart reigned over the mind, defying logic and reason and like a train, until it had traveled the distance of a lonely track, had switched its course, there would be only the journey to the love curdled within. Plain and simple, he wasn't Anwar. The thrill and excitement of a new relationship could be refreshing though. But loving Randy would be a conscious effort. With Anwar it had been natural. But love and happiness was desirable also. Randy could give that. In the end that would be all that mattered. Once inside the house, she leaned on her door and thought about how she kissed him. Just *what had* her kiss told him?

Chapter 14
Bull's Eye!

The tunnel vision was back again. He was searching equally as hard for new and relevant information as he was for possessions that belonged to Buddy. Whatever he would find of value would be appreciated and had to be discovered soon. Time was passing by quickly. So many interruptions had swallowed up his research time and it was so uncanny how things had happened. He needed a miracle and apparently Marie Laveau had decided not to lend him a hand. He was on his own. He hadn't believed she would.

He went to jazz societies, organizations and academies and spoke with them about Buddy and his intent to find something of substance. But so many of them were run by other races and nationalities and they were not about to break their necks to help tell the world that the first jazz musician in America had been black and that jazz had African roots. He couldn't understand how the genre of jazz had changed its face so rapidly from having been taught and dominated mostly by black people to being taught and dominated by so many others. Were black people abandoning jazz to create new genres of music and not returning to it? Had it been left alone to be adopted by everyone else like an orphan child? He hoped blacks would swarm back to their music in groves just as they did when Buddy's horn had called them home years ago. Until then he would have to be selective as to where he would seek information. He had already denoted anger in other groups whenever he spoke upon Buddy having been the first jazz musician in America. They hadn't wanted to be reminded.

Even while searching nonstop, nothing showed up. Nothing. Anwar had become so frustrated that he thought about leaving for home early. He thought back to a time when he wanted to drop out of grad school but his father had stressed to him that 'a quitter never wins and a winner never quits.' This small morsel of wisdom and truth inspired him again and he decided he'd give himself a little more time.

A senior high rise was located directly behind a park. Several elderly people wandered about feeding pigeons, carrying on conversations with grandchildren, and playing checkers and dominos. He asked the elders about Buddy and if they had ever heard his music? They'd all heard of Buddy and some had sworn their grandparents had danced to Buddy's music. Some told him short tales of Storyville that they'd heard or they spoke about their careers as jazz singers or musicians. Some sang jazz ballads to him and were great singers. They had 'missed their calling.' But nobody knew anyone who owned a cylinder of Buddy's.

One day while interviewing in that same park, he ran into a happy go lucky fellow appearing to be in his early thirties. The man had been standing in the parking lot making fresh talk to the ladies that passed by as vintage jazz poured through his car speakers. He was a big guy with a large round head and a baby face. He made a little twist or bow with the music but nobody really paid him any attention. He was just having himself a good time, loving and living life and he didn't expect the women to take him seriously but felt a need to meet their acquaintances just the same.

"Hey, my brotha," Anwar said in a friendly tone, "I see you dig the old jazz sounds. You hip to Buddy Bolden? You know anyone that owns a cylinder by Buddy?"

"Buddy Bolden? Wait a minute—yes, sure. I remember my grandmother said that her grandmother played his music. She called him King Buddy Bolden. He was the love of my great-great Gran's life."

"Your great-great gran?"

"Of course she's not with us any longer but my Grandma's still living. Want me to take you to see her?" That was like 'jazz' to Anwar's ears.

"Hell yeah, brother. Would you mind taking me today?"

"Well, I'll have to call her first."

The man darted to the pay phone a few yards away and returned after a minute or two.

"It's alright. She welcomes you. Mind if I ride with you? My tank's a little low."

Maybe Anwar should have been suspicious but he was too excited to be distrustful of the man. He paid him back the quarter he used in the phone and they went down the road talking about jazz and practically every notable jazz musician. The man's name was Art.

"What do you think of Miles, Anwar?"

"Intense. He absorbed himself completely."

"And Bird?"

"Another world, man."

"Yeah."

"How bout Satch?"

"Sweet. That horn talked to ya?"

"Coltrane?"

"Aw now, that was the man."

"Hey, check this out," Art said with a smirk. "I came back home about four years ago to fix up my parents old house, right? Then. . . the love bug bit me and I haven't been back to California yet, man. My woman *lives* with me now. I didn't intend for that to happen. I don't even know how it happened. But I feel married all the time now. All the time," he whined.

Anwar laughed and followed up with, "gee I'm sorry to hear that, Bro." Then they both admitted that women had some kind of power that drove them outta their minds.

"Man, I don't know," Art said, "but if I ever get outta this one, uh uh, no more for me. I'll be a ladies man; just hit it and quit it." Anwar overstood that.

A section of the city was new to Anwar. Art told him that some of the buildings dated back hundreds of years just like the structures in the French Quarters. Several boasted artsy sculptures and wrought iron fixtures. Art explained African slaves had made the sculptures and most of the wrought iron designs with a technique that had been developed in Africa. Anwar imagined a tall, strongly built Zulu warrior standing victoriously on a lawn and with one surge of strength, breaking the chains and shackles that bound him; then running so fast that he kept up with the car. He had to blink to make sure it had only been his imagination. He didn't know if he could trust his mind after that vision or whatever the hell it had been that followed that punch in the jaw. Could Buddy have experienced that type of vision before he lost his mind?

"Hey, there you go. Pull on over to the right. Move up a little. That's good. This is it," Art said, pointing at a small structure that looked more like a storefront than anything else.

The house was pitifully framed. It was almost a shack, definitely not inviting but that was just the outside. The interior had to be a lot better. Hopefully. The most distinguishing things on the outside were the large address numbers and the pink lace curtains.

'Would there be a little old lady inside with a cower hump'? Anwar wondered. 'Would she be shrunken, and wearing a black dress with a white bodice, be silver haired and very wrinkled'? If so, she'd serve tea in delicate china that was only used for guests. There would be the scent of kitty litter and the teacakes would be hard and dusty, of course, and he'd have to fake they were delicious while she would reminisce her adventures of when she was a girl.

Art had a key and unlocked the front door. Although the sun was shining, the room was dull and the pink curtains were the only things that gave the room personality.

"Grandma! Hey baby! Where you at?"

A little dark woman emerged from the kitchen area dressed in navy blue pants, a white pullover and a gray lightweight sweater with huge pockets and white sneakers. She walked quickly for a woman her age but she took tiny steps. She was bent over a bit too, yet, she had no resemblance to the woman Anwar had conjured up in his mind. She had a tiny afro and instead of wrinkles on her face, there was only a slight dimpling in her cheeks and a little sag around her jawbone.

"Grandma, this is the brotha I told you about," Art said as he pointed to Anwar.

"Well, hello son. It's so nice to meet someone that's a keeper of black culture."

'Keeper of black culture? Now this little lady was up on what was happening,' Anwar thought.

The lady opened the door to a room near the back entrance and let out a small whining dog. "He's on punishment for chewing up my belt. I hope you've learned your lesson," she said, scolding the dog that actually seemed to understand her.

"Listen. Do you mind if we take a little walk? Woody's got to use the bathroom."

"Oh, that's fine with me."

"I'll wait here," Art said, as he ate the remainder of greens from the large pot on the stove.

Anwar reached down and rubbed the little dog's head. It barked and growled at him.

"Woody! Stop that. Bad dog," the lady scolded. "He's really upset with me and taking it out on you."

Woody whined a little then scurried from one side of the pavement to the other sniffing and peeing along the way.

"Oh, my name is Anwar." He shook the woman's hand then fanned through the pages in his notebook.

"Well, pleased to meet you, Anwar. I'm going to straighten out my grandson for not introducing me properly. 'Grandma'. That's the only name he thinks I have but I'm really Ruth McKay. It was Randall years and years ago. And you're not from here, are you? You speak like you're from the north."

"I'm originally from Connecticut."

"That's all the way on the East Coast! I always thought the person that came would be from here. Oh, you're probably asking yourself, 'what is this old lady babbling about?' I am talking about Buddy, don't worry. But I guess you're the one he chose so I won't bother it."

"I'm not sure I understand."

"Well, I'll get to that."

She and Anwar broke the ice quickly. She told him about the historical research she'd been collecting about Goree Island and her dedication and plans to continue teaching neighborhood children their African heritage at a small bookstore until she had joined the ancestors.

"I've always wondered why our history before slavery is still unknown amongst so many of our people," Anwar said.

"That's been by design. You see, it would be so empowering that it would uplift our race. It's been standard practice in America to hold our people down and few groups other than black people care about empowering our youth. I always tell our children that black people did not fall out of the sky as slaves. We had an illustrious history that was *interrupted by slavery*. I feel as an elder, I have an obligation to teach them Ancient Black History. Public schools teach Greek, European, and even Asian history but very few schools teach African history. I also let them know that we didn't choose to leave our land and that African Americans are the only people in this country besides indigenous people that *are not immigrants*. Of course, there is evidence now that African people came to America thousands of years ago but the majority of our African people were dragged here by gunpoint against their will and enslaved for hundreds of years. We played an enormous role in building this country. Nobody tells them that. But slavery killed our knowledge of self and we must learn who we are again. The Honorable Marcus Garvey said 'a people without the knowledge of their past history, origin and culture is like a tree without roots.' And it's true.' Oh, I meant to warn you, I'm quite militant."

"That's not militancy, that's truth. That's why I'm here doing research," Anwar replied. "It's all for the truth."

"Yes. And. . . ," she began, "things black people have invented have not been credited to them. We weren't permitted to hold patents for hundreds of years so somebody else took the credit. And some groups to this day are still trying to discredit black people from being the original builders of ancient Egypt and it's so ridiculous because the evidence is right in their faces. Most researchers and scientists have put aside the prejudices and confirmed that Egypt was an ancient black civilization. Of course, other groups of people migrated to that region later on but

Egypt was built by black African people. They say some archaeologists were so distraught about those findings that they destroyed the black features on a lot of the statues and artifacts to mislead humanity. You ever notice that the noses and the fullest parts of the lips are missing on a lot of Egyptian sculptures?" Ruth added. Anwar had and he knew why. "History books will tell you that Napaleon was so upset to discover the Sphinx had been built by black people that he fired cannon balls to destroy it. He didn't ruin it entirely. It's still standing and it still looks African."

"Who else would make their art look like black people but black people? It's real simple. It's one of those common sense things but science backs it up too," Anwar said.

"You're right. I've been to Egypt six times and it's so obvious it was designed and created by black Africans. And the descendants of those Africans are still there. Some people might say 'what does it matter who built Egypt?' But it matters a great deal to a people who are always being scorned and discredited for their contributions. Some people don't even want to accept the fact that Egypt is a country in Africa. They want to take it completely out of Africa and make it stand alone. And that's why I have a passion for teaching the truth. And our children need to know about the other black civilizations too, not just Egypt. There's Nubia, Mali, Dahomey, Benin, Angola, Songhai, and so many more. We're researching ancient Black Nubia now. It was nearly identical to Egypt in culture. Scientists say it was at least five-hundred years older than Egypt and the pyramids were built far more superior. It's been written in some history books that the Nubians eventually migrated and began building Egypt. As a matter of fact that is being written in the most reputable magazines too. I was shocked. I guess most scientists say, what's the point in fabricating things? It won't ever change the truth. And the truth is such a noble thing. It will always come out."

Anwar, shook his head slowly, "We're the Cinderellas of the earth just like Duke said. That's Duke Ellington."

"I know what Duke you mean."

"Yeah, of course you do. But in other words, the ones you discredit most are the very ones that are loaded with the gifts and talents and have made some of the greatest contributions."

"That's right. Now tell me more about yourself. Who is this Anwar that suddenly showed up at my doorstep?"

He told her that he was a bassist and spoke about Merriam and his new job as a professor.

"I was a public school teacher," she said. "I taught sewing. That's an old craft now but back then you weren't considered a lady of the marrying kind unless you were domestic. Girls were taught to want marriage in my day. I wanted to teach history but my parents told me that I should leave that job to the men. Well I did and I'm sorry that I didn't fight for what I wanted. Look. There are benches over there. Let's sit and talk."

They crossed the street and headed toward the benches.

"I have a surprise for you," she said with a little sly smile.

"For me? Really?"

"Oh yes. I've been waiting for you to come along for years and when I got that call today from Art. . . Oh, can you run and save us some seats?"

Anwar ran ahead. The paper in his notebook fanned and flipped and flapped as he tossed it on a bench. He reached it just before a group of teenagers would've claimed it. With one foot resting on it he lit a cigarette, took a few puffs, inhaling deeply then stomped it out before Ruth arrived. But she stopped a few feet from him to watch the small children race back and forth. She appeared to be reminiscing, possibly about Art or her own children.

"Just look at the wonders of life," she said with great passion. "They have little bitty hands and feet and mouths and noses and organs and those little body parts actually work. That is a miracle. You must know that though. I believe all lovers of jazz have realized the miracles. Oh now, what do you need to know about Buddy?"

"Well, first of all I get this funny feeling whenever I stand someplace that Buddy had been. I believe it's ancestral or spiritual." Ruth's smile stretched wilder and wider as he spoke.

"He knows you're researching him. Buddy was very sensitive, my grandmother said. Maybe to a fault."

"Yeah, I'm sure. But I just wanted to mention that. But anyway, I have this obsession to introduce Buddy's geniustude to the world. I just don't have anything to crystallize his music or character. I know things have already been discovered but I believe there's more."

"Oh there is," Ruth said, confidently.

"You know that for sure?"

"Buddy was an innovative and productive man."

"That he was. So how did your grandmother know Buddy?"

Ruth gave him that old smile again as though she might have been talking to a child. Well, she was more than twice his age. Maybe he was a child.

"Well let's just say she knew him well. That was before he got married. Maybe married. It had been rumored that he was married. My grandmother's name was Charlotte Badeaux. She loved Buddy terribly and way before he had acquired any fame but her father forbid she see him. Back then not many people thought highly of musicians and especially Buddy because he was far from the model musician. He played jazz. And later, he played it in the red light district. Jazz was scandalous because it had black African roots. We had been taught to hate it by white society during slavery. Not even blood relatives would associate with black jazz musicians. Now Buddy had already acquired a little reputation with the women. That wasn't a good thing although my grandmother hadn't cared but her father did. And he had a terrible time keeping her away from Buddy. They say Buddy was incredibly handsome and he was tall and well built. Gran said once a woman fought two other women over Buddy. One was trying to carry his horn, the other his coat, but that woman wouldn't allow it. Women adored him. Buddy was Gran's King, even though they were only friends after he got married. Oh, by the way, that's what the people called him, you know, 'King Buddy Bolden'."

"Yeah, I know. And I've heard about the ladies."

"I believe some of them would have done anything for him. Gran said some might have gone into the brothels if he'd asked them. He was just that charming and he knew it. Anyway, a lot of other black musicians stopped playing other genres because they had heard what Buddy was playing and admired his courage. Buddy didn't care if people called it the 'devil's music,' and other black musicians stopped caring too. Pretty soon practically all the musicians in New Orleans, black and white were imitating Buddy. His style was being played at this club and that club, in the 'French Quarters or Vieux Carre'— Some clubs the poor boy wasn't even allowed to go into because of the color of his skin. But everybody could go into black clubs and they did. They learned black music and took it with them. And that was how a lot of our music and credits got away from us."

"Yeah. And that went on from the onset of slavery."

"And so many other people claimed to have created jazz. I believe Buddy was especially frustrated over that and it played a large role in his excessive drinking." Ruth shuddered. "I couldn't imagine that happening to anyone."

"That's a bitter pill to swallow. And he probably didn't get proper psychiatric care either. Today there are meds that are very effective in treating mental illness."

"Oh yes. But there were probably a few other things that piled up on Buddy too and, well, he just snapped. But when Buddy would play, oh ho ho, black people couldn't help but dance. Of course our dancing had African roots so it was called immoral and frowned upon. This country didn't understand African culture back then and it still doesn't. But all Buddy's jazz was not to dance to. Some of it was moody and reflective and took the listener's mind to other places, like blues does. Blues was called 'nigger and devil's music' too. But now everybody sings and plays our blues. Isn't that something? And a lot of other people that played our blues and jazz around the world never told where they had learned it so people in other lands had no idea it had black roots til they found out for themselves. Some people were honest and admitted where they'd learned it but not many. You know, I think my next subject at the bookstore will be on jazz."

"That's a very worthy subject," Anwar said approvingly.

"Now during slavery we were stripped of our drums and dance and everything else we brought with us all around the country but not here. We were able to assert our culture in some areas. But I believe one reason a lot of slave owners didn't strip our ancestors of all our culture was because they were fascinated by it. People would gather around to watch our ancestors drum and dance and perform rituals and sing on Congo Square. And our ancestors were resplendent as they showed off their costumes, their masks and feathers and trinkets. Oh! Historians have even written about them on Congo Square. Tourists are fascinated over our church services the same way today. They line up at the door and some even pay to get inside but they're taking our culture back with them.

Other nationalities have already started to sing black gospel and have started arranging their choir music just like ours. Some of their churches have worship and praise services like black churches in America now. People are even starting to imitate our styles of singing. And dancing. It's the same old story. Other groups see something very rich in our culture even if they don't admit it. And I say it's alright to share cultures but don't discredit the inventors. We sing opera, we play Bach and we perform ballet and kung fu but we're not claiming ownership of those things and we don't wish to discredit any group. So tell me, what is it called when one scorns a people because of what they create then turns around and imitates it?" Ruth asked.

"I don't even have an answer for that. But what bothers me most is that there are people who have gone as far as producing books and films full of lies to try to discredit us. I keep running into that," Anwar stated.

"Which is why we must continue to document our own history no matter what. But I believe the world is learning the truth now. But that old slave master just couldn't fathom 'black folks' having all that creativity and talent. And Egypt, Nubia and our other African civilizations literally knocked some folks off their feet," Ruth chuckled.

"Yeah, they sure did. Listen, did your grandmother have any pictures of Buddy?" Anwar asked abruptly, almost rudely.

"Oh, goodness yes! Gran's brother worked with a well known photographer. Buddy used him quite frequently to take pictures of him playing in the dance halls. I just don't know what happened to all the pictures. You know she was always afraid somebody would find them. My mother said she had looked at them often with gran. And gran told her that Buddy played that cornet so loud. People used to worry about him bursting his head wide open. And some thought something did erupt in his brain while he was playing. Recently, I read where certain sound waves could damage the brain. And nobody could play a horn as loud as Buddy, she said. And it was so sad how his mind just left him so completely. He never got well and he was only twenty-nine. Isn't that sad what happened to him?"

"Yeah. I've thought about that for years. So did he do anything else in his spare time? I doubt if there were a lot of other places to go besides clubs back then. Maybe to a park or something."

"Oh, Buddy socialized. He drank and talked a lot of trash as you young people say. He hung out at his friend's barbershop. He moved fast and could jump nearly eight feet high."

"Wow. Did she keep up with him to his death?"

"No. She had to let him go after he was committed. His mind was just—gone. People thought he had contracted syphilis at first. It was going around pretty heavily back then. But Buddy didn't have it. They claimed he had alcohol dementia but I believe he was too young to have had that. I'm convinced it was the theft of his music that drove him mad. But a few people thought someone worked roots on Buddy." She looked at Anwar and smiled. "But I don't suppose you believe in voodoo, do you?"

"I visited Marie Laveau's tomb."

"Oh, then you believe maybe."

"Yeah. . ., not really. What about Buddy's cylinder?"

"Grandmother played it maybe three times or so. My mother and I could hear the music coming from Grandmother's room. I think she only had one cylinder, maybe two. I don't remember but after awhile she stopped playing the music. I don't really know what happened to the cylinders. Things get lost through the years."

"Man! That's what I was hoping to find before my sabbatical was up. Do you know anyone else that dealt with Buddy?"

"Well, I always thought the Gifford's did. Old Man Gifford was one of my grandmother's friends. He died almost the same time as my grandmother. I went to school with his grandson, Jim. He inherited the family house. I forget the name of the street but I have the address written down somewhere. Now I believe the Gifford's were Creole and surprisingly that family had a lot of power in those days. I'm sure Jim Gifford still lives there. People don't move out of those houses. Now let's see—I was born in 1927, my mother was born in 1908 and my grandmother was born in 1880. The last time she played that cylinder I had to be about fifteen years old. It was about 19. . . um. . . 1942."

'That's it? That was all the lady had to tell me? That was nothing', Anwar thought. 'All that running around for nothing.' He was disappointed in Art. His grandmother gave him only history and stories about Buddy. He didn't have time to waste like that. He sighed and slowly reached for his notebook.

"Oh, my goodness! I don't want to forget these, Anwar."

She reached into her large sweater pocket and pulled out four yellowed envelopes in plastic pouches. Two had been addressed to Charles Bolden from Charlotte Badeaux and the other two were addressed to Charlotte Badeaux from Charles Bolden. Anwar froze as if he were paralyzed. Ruth forced the letters into his hands and he just sat very still, clutching them.

"Billetdoux, love letters. They were written before anyone discovered they knew one another. I've never known what they said to each other. Never read them. But they're yours. I had put them in my will to go to one of our jazz centers but I really wanted to give them to someone that came to me, someone that was looking for something of Buddy's and here you are. You'll have to be careful though. They're falling apart. They're over a hundred years old. I tried to preserve them by keeping them out of the light but I suppose that didn't help much. They would break apart if you tried to read them."

'They can be restored', he thought. There were several methods used to restore old documents. Anwar had seen how it was done in the library's photo collection department when he was a page.

"I just ask that you do this for me," Ruth continued. "Place them in a museum or institution that is owned and operated by our people. I'd like for them to stay in New Orleans and in a black neighborhood since Buddy was a black man. Too many of our youth have not been exposed to their own culture. I just wanted to put them in the hands of someone who had the same kind of passion and love for Buddy that I did, then let that person take control. But I sure didn't think you'd be from the East Coast. Isn't that strange? This city is bursting with jazz researchers. I'm inclined to think that Buddy had something to do with you being here and I wouldn't put anything past our voodoo queen either. Now I want you to take my phone number"

'They still believe that stuff,' Anwar thought as he kissed Ruth over and over on her baby soft cheek. With good timing, an ice cream truck drove up to a crowd of children and he offered her an ice cream cone. She accepted and he paid for all the children's cones too, thirteen in all. Like two people in love, he and Ruth headed back hand in hand eating ice cream with Woody sniffing along. He'd made more progress that day than he had in all the months he'd been in New Orleans. A piece of Buddy was in his possession. He couldn't share that with Beard until he had made it back home. He really wanted to but Beard would get too emotional and that would not be good for his heart.

"Tomorrow's Saturday and a good time to give Gifford a visit. Tell him I sent you," Ruth said, as she scribbled out an address. They said goodbye as though they were parting as best friends, hugging and squeezing one another to death. Anwar promised he would visit the following summer.

"I would love that. Nobody spends much time with me anymore except this one who comes to eat up all my food."

"You shouldn't cook so good," Art returned, winking his eye at Anwar. He kissed his grandmother and the men climbed into the van and off they went. Anwar thanked Art over and over and left him with a full tank of gas and cash for his pocket.

He called Merriam as soon as he'd gotten home. She was elated and wanted to fly down to celebrate.

"NO! Umm, no Merriam, that won't be necessary, honey."

"Why'd you say 'no' like that?"

"I just did Merriam, no reason. I'll be home sometime next week, okay?"

"You *should* be eager to see me. What's going on?"

"Nothing," Anwar answered flatly.

"I hope you're not lying. You promise you'll be back next week?"

"I promise, unless I run into something else."

"Okay. Ain't misbehavin'. Still love you," she purred.

"Love you too, babe."

Had he still loved Merriam, he wondered? The absence had made them grow apart and he was not even sure that he wanted a steady girl anymore. Maybe if Merriam was more like Stanza he would desire the relationship. Yet, Merriam did bring balance to his world. Could Stanza have brought balance or chaos? That's something he would never know unless__

Forget it! 'Let Stanza stay where she is,' he thought. He was not about to reach out to her again.

He checked in with Giles but he didn't tell him about

Buddy's letters. That would be dessert once he had returned. It was still unbelievable that he had the letters. Who manipulated that? Buddy or the Queen? . . . Or was it just destiny? Would he ever know? But he felt like roaming the world forever discovering and piecing together black history. He had convinced himself that he was pretty good at it.

Chapter 15
Double Bull's Eye!

Jim Gifford lived in a huge plantation house proto-
typical of the old south. Gifford's great grandmother had
been the mistress of his white great-grandfather who had
owned the home and land. Plaçage, a legal system in New
Orleans allowed young white men, usually those that had
not yet become financially established, to legally choose a
slave girl of color from 12 years and up to act as a consort or
partner until he could accumulate the finances to support a
white wife. Some white men never did get married but kept
their plaçagees and had children with them as they would a
wife. Other men would maintain two households thus
move their plaçagees to another area of town and support
them and the children. The offspring of these women of
color and their partners were born free. Most often these
women were quadroons, the offspring of a mulatto and a
white person. Jim Gifford's great grandmother was a
quadroon plaçagee and had bore her partner several
children. Why New Orleans ordained this system is a
mystery in itself. Some say it was only because it was illegal
for white men to have sexual relations with white women
until they had married them but other researchers surmised
that those white men were attracted to the African female
physicality still detectable in quadroons. Then some
researchers determined that it was due to economics, stating
that a white man could demand higher prices at the auction
block for light colored children he'd fathered with his

plaçagee. Yet, race mixing was also said to have been illegal, so the system was a bit of a mystery in itself.

The Gifford's house had tall columns and a wide gated entrance. Trees lined up on each side of the walkway. The huge front yard was unkempt and there was a lot of land in the back that seemed to consist mostly of sun scorched grass.

Anwar lifted the heavy iron rapper and brought it down on the door but no one answered. He knocked several more times but still no answer. Just as he pulled out a pen to scribble a note, a young boy about ten years old appeared.

"You lookin' for Grandpa?"

"Ummm, yes, I suppose. Mr. Gifford?"

"He went to the grocery store. He'll be back. The store is right down the street. The family is in there in the back. They can't hear you though. This door is thick. Want me to take you in?"

"No. I can wait right out here for him. Thanks son."

The boy left Anwar on the front porch smoking a cigarette. Not long afterwards, a large four-door sedan very similar to his father's car pulled in front of the house and a man who appeared to be in his mid to late seventies moved toward the gate that actually stretched several yards from the house's front entrance.

Anwar left the porch to give Mr. Gifford a hand with his bags. The spry old man gave them to him willingly without question.

"They stop parkin' in the driveway all crooked, I wouldn't have to park out front like that. That's what happens when you got grown folks all around ya. They got no respect for the aged," he fussed.

"Oh, you don't look so old."

Gifford stopped and stared at Anwar. "And who might you be, may I ask?"

I'm Anwar Rasual, sir. Mrs. McKay sent me."

"Mrs. Mckay? You mean Ruth? I know Ruth. Haven't heard from her in over a year. Something wrong?"

"No, nothing's wrong. She just told me that maybe you can help me with something. I'm a professor from Connecticut and I'm doing research on Buddy Bolden. I'm trying to come up with something new that had never been discovered for the archives of jazz. She said you might know something about his wax cylinder."

"Why should I know about that? I didn't know Bolden, my people did," he said, rubbing his wooly gray hair.

"Well, she said that just in case you were still in the house that—

"No. I don't know nothin' about Bolden. Don't have nothing." Then he added, "some white men came around asking questions about Bolden a long time ago and wanted to look in our attic and basement. We told them 'no'. We don't trust white people. I might be a little light skinned myself but that don't mean I'm white."

Anwar smiled and walked with the little feisty man to his door. Gifford stopped to knock on practically every tree that led the way and before he entered the house he faced the east and bowed.

"Come on in, young man," he said, proudly.

The interior was splendid. Gifford walked through like a king. There were several children in one room hovered over a board game on the beautiful oak floor and the smell of bacon still lingered in the air.

"You can have a seat. Two of my daughters and they husbands and six of my grandbabies stay with me. We got ten bedrooms. We shut half the house off when the weather gets cooler. It stays warmer that way. Not too many houses are in good condition like this one anymore. Wanna tour?"

Gifford led Anwar up the long, wide mahogany staircase. He looked in each room carefully, actually searching for something that might be old enough to belong to Buddy. The furnishings could use replacing, but the floors didn't creak much. The walls hadn't cracked and even most of the windowpanes were original. After the tour, he and Gifford sat down in the large living room. Gifford's daughter offered Anwar lemonade and a teacake and he accepted. One of Gifford's granddaughters had just finished polishing an antique clock.

"We always got a lot to do here," the granddaughter explained, as she placed the clock on the mantelpiece. "We ain't rich where we can hire maids." The girl then grabbed a broom and swept around the room.

Gifford yelled, "take that broom outta here!"

"Oh Granpa! You're too old fashioned," she snapped.

As she was leaving, the broom swept lightly over Gifford's feet. He had a fit. "Lemme have that broom! Now!" He practically snatched it out of the young lady's hand and spit on the broom's curling straw, turned it around and spit on the other side. "Don't need to be going to jail."

"Granpa, you're too superstitious."

"You just be careful where you sweep. And don't forget we got company." The granddaughter left the room shaking her head.

The Giffords house was as immaculate as Merriam's. He swept crumbs and the tiniest particles of lint and dust off the table with his hands. There were several family pictures and artifacts on the wall and Anwar rose to examine them. Portraits dated back to the early eighteen hundreds.

"That white man there? That's great-great grandfather, Newton," Gifford explained. "He got my great-great grandmother from the quadroon ballroom when she was only fifteen years old. She lived right in this house with his wife and took care of his wife cause she kept having miscarriages and issues of blood. She finally died and then my great-

great grandfather died like twenty years later and he left her this house."

"It's a fine house," Anwar added.

"That it is," Gifford said proudly. "A lot of my people have lived here. It's the family home. Mostly African slaves built it. They say my great-great grandmother freed all the slaves and they lived like a big family right here. But after awhile she had to pass for white and act like she owned black slaves cause a lot of people wanted to own this house. She was tough and didn't take nothin' off nobody. They used to say I was just like her except I'm a little mean. But I have to be. People keep trying to take this house over and over again. Things like that will make you mean. Wasn't my fault my family got this house. They deserved it as hard as they had to work. And it wasn't my fault my great-great grandmother outsmarted them to keep this land. But they best to leave us alone now cause my son-in-law is into politics. He knows a lot of powerful people."

"Well, good for you. Hold on to your home. And speaking of home, that's where I'll be headed soon. I just hate to go back without Buddy's cylinder."

The more Anwar spoke of his musical passions, Gifford seemed more relaxed, as though he had let go of something that had been haunting him.

Anwar rose to leave after about an hour of aimless chatter. No longer did he feel he had the makings of a great historian. The men shook hands and as he made his way down the stairs. He felt as though he had failed a great task. He thought that a researcher had to fight the temptation to add or fabricate anything for the actual findings were so very few. But before he reached the gate, Gifford called him back.

"I have something you might be interested in. Not all houses in New Orleans was built with cellars cause the

165

ground is so moist. But our house got a cellar, a good one."

Anwar entered the house again and Gifford took him into a fancy alcove with a door that led to the cellar.

"Grab a pair of those gloves. Ya ought not to be touching nothing with ya bare hands. We probably breeding bacteria down there. I know we got rats. I set traps and poison out but they just leave and come right back."

"There are only two windows in this cellar. They're both in the front. There's nothing in the back. My people use to make wine and store it in here til they could sell it. They kept it cool and dark. That's how they wanted it. Cool and dark."

"I bet it is dark with just the two windows."

"It's dark but it's not damp. This house got built on the driest part of the city and my other son-in-law said this house got a cellar inside a cellar. How bout that? He's a smart young man. He's gonna be a architect and he knows his stuff," Gifford said, proudly.

They reached a little table and Gifford took up a portable lamp and flicked it on. It was very powerful. Finally they found their way into the cellar. The ceiling was a little less than six feet high and Anwar had to lower his head as they made their way through. It reminded him of a crawl space and it was cool and dark just like Gifford said. Surprisingly, it didn't smell too much like mildew. His parent's basement had a stronger mildew smell than Gifford's.

"Listen, Gifford started, "I think God gave you a good heart to do the right thing. I don't mean the go to church kinda thing. I don't do religion myself. I'm too much a independent thinker. I believe in God and tries to live right and that's bout as much as I can see I need. I ain't the type to have no preachers shoutin' and pointin' they fingers in my face like they perfect. It takes a good heart to get in heaven, anyway, not no sermon. An' I think you got a good heart an' that's why I'm gonna show you something."

They continued to walk through the cellar. Cobwebs and empty wine racks hung from the low ceilings. Saddles and bridles were strewn in corners and a small plow leaned against a door. They stopped at a dust ridden shelf. Gifford handed the light to Anwar as he fumbled with his keys. He unlocked the door. There was a loud *'squeak* when he pushed it open and Anwar immediately thought of murder mysteries.

"I don't know what's here. I never really wanted to look through all these things. Shoulda. But looking back, I remember this is where my grandfather put a lot of his personal stuff. Ms. Charlotte had stuff in this room too. I remember her name was written on something. Did Ruth tell you 'bout her grandmother and Buddy?" Anwar nodded 'yes'.

"Well, her and Buddy stayed friends I guess til he dropped out of society. I don't know what else they mighta did and wasn't nobody's bizness. I suppose they were real special to each other. My peoples knew all about em. Said they loved Ms. Charlotte and knew if her daddy hadn't been so mean she mighta been the one Buddy had for keeps."

Gifford took the powerful light and moved its beam from wall to wall. "Must be over here."

Anwar followed Gifford to the back of the room where he aimed the light on a top shelf. Barely visible on a high shelf was the name 'Charlotte,' written on a dusty linen sheet that covered several items. A shift to the left and there was a square metal box half covered with a very dusty cloth.

"I can't reach that high no more. Take the light and grab those things off that shelf. Careful. Get that one too."

The beam of light went here and there while Anwar grabbed as best he could. Finally, Gifford grabbed the light.

"Come on. Let's get outta here. I never stayed down here too long. Like I said, there are rats in this cellar. I ain't talking bout mice. I mean rats!"

Anwar followed Gifford back upstairs. The kids and one of his daughters had been standing at the landing waiting, wondering what was going on.

"Com' on," Gifford said to them, "git outta the way."

He led Anwar to a large enclosed porch. The boxes had been heavy and he sat them down right before he would have dropped them.

Gifford yelled for the children and his daughter to stop being so nosy. He pulled the porch door closed and locked it. The children still peeped from a window that was positioned at an angle in an adjoining room.

"The bad thing bout ya kids livin' wit ya is ya don't get a bit of privacy. Got gran'babies running all 'round but I shouldn't complain, I guess. I woulda been daid if they hadn't been here to get me to the hospital. I had a stroke two years ago. My wife had one five years ago. We buried her last year." He changed the subject quickly.

"Alright, ya might as well unwrap that one first. I don't know, but I believe all this was Ms. Charlotte's stuff. My peoples didn't go in that room too much. It's spooky down there, tell the truth." Anwar nodded 'yes.'

He didn't believe much would come of their adventure so without any caution he simply slipped the dust covered cloth off the heavy case, being careful not to spill the large rat droppings. They coughed and hacked so badly from the dust that they had to pull their shirts over their faces. After the dust settled Anwar slowly opened the largest metal case and removed an item that was wrapped in blue cloth. He just sat staring. All he could do was look at Gifford. He smiled approvingly.

"That it, ain't it? That's what ya been looking for?"

Anwar's voice was gravelly and high-pitched as he said,

'yes.' He had removed from the case the phonograph that played wax cylinders.

"How bout that thing there? Hey, ya alright?"

Anwar gave a slight nod. He felt lightheaded but this was not a time to faint so he moved to the other box and removed the cover. He tilted back and fell to the floor. Inscribed on the boxes were, *Buddy Bolden.* There they were. Two cylinders. He could barely breathe.

Gifford suddenly appeared nervous as he watched Anwar struggle for his breath. He felt as though he had done something he had no business doing.

Anwar composed himself and began to breathe rhythmically again. "It's alright, man. These are what the world needs. These are good things, great things."

Somehow Buddy had gained possession of his own music. 'Could it be,' Anwar wondered, 'that the recording company gave the cylinders to him because it did not think jazz music would go very far? And if that were the case, why would they have bothered to record Buddy at all? Could Ashanti have been right when she said people in the area often had the recordings of local studios that went out of business? Or could Buddy have purchased the cylinders himself? But Buddy was a poor musician. Did somebody buy them for him? Did a friend or better yet, a female friend buy them for him? That too was very possible.'

A box in the same metal case as the cylinders had been filled with personal items. It contained costume jewelry and notions. He discovered yet, a smaller box, yellow in color with a beautiful decorative ivory border. He opened it slowly and carefully and there he saw something wonderful. Photographs. He counted fifty-three in all. Sixteen were of Buddy, his band, and his friends. At that moment the world had ceased to exist.

Gifford didn't ask to be paid for the items just as Ruth hadn't. They didn't want money. They both had been more concerned with sharing the items.

"These things don't belong to my family," Gifford explained. "They belong to our peoples."

All Gifford asked of Anwar was that he place the items where the whole world could see the greatness of a man. Anwar promised him that he would. He left with his heart pounding fiercely.

He called Ruth and told her the news. She could barely hear him because of Woody's barking.

"Oh, he's driving me crazy today. There are men working next door. Quiet Woody, quiet! Now what did you say?" She asked loudly.

"I said I have two of Buddy's cylinders, the phonograph and more pictures and I can't thank you enough."

There was silence on the line and finally Ruth said, "I don't know where to begin. I am so happy for Buddy and I never doubted you would find the cylinder. Cylinders. I'll have to sit down after this news. Oh my! I'll let Art know. Now you be safe and call me when you get home."

When he called Ron and Ashanti to tell them about the cylinders, they said, "Marie Laveau." He just chuckled.

The ride back to the apartment was slow and cautious. Anwar kept wondering about the cylinders and how they'd gotten in the Gifford cellar. That would always remain a mystery and the biggest mystery would be how he wound up with Buddy's things period. But hadn't that been what he had gone to New Orleans to find?

Obviously Buddy knew about protecting the cylinders because he had Ruth's grandmother store them where they wouldn't meet with light or heat. Sadly enough, it hadn't crossed any of their minds that Buddy would never return.

The cylinders had been stored inside a box with a tight fitting lid similar to some brands of oatmeal boxes. Anwar inspected them with a very dim light. They seemed to have been covered with a thin moldy film. Both were about eight inches high and shaped like a spool of thread. They had grooves in them similar to those in a 78 LP. Anwar cleaned the cylinders with safety swabs and his fingertips, lifting away as much stringy mold as possible. He also cleaned and oiled the phonograph. Would it play the cylinders? It should. But had Buddy been told to hold back on the jazz? Was he instructed to play something else? Could he bare it if that were the case? No. The music had to be jazz. He would listen to it with Giles. Then Beard. Afterwards, the music would be duplicated and he would return Buddy's relics to his sisters and brothers of New Orleans. He knew Buddy would want it no other way.

Chapter 16
Home And The Stranger

The van was loaded carefully for the ride back home. He drove the rental because he couldn't risk losing the relics on the plane or train. A sad yearning for Stanza accompanied his ride. He would probably never see her again. But Buddy had been on his mind too much to give a lot of thought to the beautiful woman that intrigued his world. But right then it was as if something deep on the inside was decaying and falling away like dead leaves as he drove further and further from the place that had given him new life.

He arrived home at about 11:00 p.m. He didn't bother to wake Merriam. Furthermore, he had been feeling strange about the whole relationship, as if he hadn't wanted it anymore.

He looked around his house and noticed that it had been cleaned to no end. Merriam. Now she had even taken away his insignia of cluttered bookshelves and overflowing ashtrays. He had a right to live that way, hadn't he?

After he had made coffee and unpacked his notebooks the latch slowly turned and the door opened. Guess who? She didn't run and hug him, overjoyed to see him home the way he had imagined she would. She was cool and aloof. It had bothered him. He looked at her interestingly. She'd lost weight. He could see her breasts through her gown. He imagined himself coming down on them, licking and sucking her nipples hungrily and he immediately obtained an erection. She slid around the back of his chair very quietly as though she were hiding something from him. He turned to watch her but then she just circled back around and sat at the table. She finally spoke. "Hi. I was up. I saw your light on. Welcome back."

"Yeah, whatever," Anwar replied dryly and upset because she didn't run to hug him and because she had been so calm.

"Lemme see your face. Hold your head up."

Anwar looked at Merriam and put on a sad baby boy face hoping that she would began kissing him all over his mouth and cheek but that didn't happen. She examined his jaw, prodded it gently and massaged it.

"I feel the scar tissue. The swelling's not too noticeable."

"Well, wait til my mother sees it."

"Oh she's gonna have a fit. You know she warned you something was going to happen."

"She warns everybody that something is going to happen."

There was a little awkwardness in the space of nothingness when Merriam suddenly broke out laughing.

"Oh, it's funny? You think it's funny?"

She couldn't stop laughing. She started and stopped a few times then finally caught her breath.

"It's not funny. It's just that you took a heck of a punch. Giles was supposed to get that punch. You know that, don't you? I told you he wasn't to be trusted."

"Let's not go there, Merriam, okay?"

"My poor Anwar. So you have his letters?" she asked with a sudden seriousness.

"Ummm hmmm. I have pictures and two cylinders and the phonograph too." Merriam sat with her mouth wide open in disbelief.

"Close your mouth before something flies in."

"But you're kidding, aren't you?"

"I'll show them to you first thing in the morning, but right now, I just want to sit."

"You're not going to try to play that phonograph by yourself are you?"

"Why not? I found it by myself."

"But you have to know what you're doing. You might ruin the cylinders."

"I'm miles ahead of you. I've had diagrams on how to operate that kind of phonograph way before I found one. Besides, I have to play it myself. That's how Buddy would want it."

He leaned back in his chair and nibbled on a pencil eraser.

"Alright now; go on and break it."

"Some things never change, do they, Merriam?"

"Well, my weight has changed."

"Yeah I noticed. Been dieting?"

"And exercising."

"I thought you looked fine the way you were."

"Yeah, well I had to move on from what you thought." She turned away and looked at the floor.

"I'm going to have a baby next year so I figured if I get thin now I won't have too much excess weight after the baby is born. Oh, please, don't look at me like that Anwar. Either you want to marry me and have a family or either you don't. It's very simple. If you don't, have no fear, because there is always somebody that will. This is not a threat, it's just the truth. I'm gonna give myself the life I want and never again will I live the life somebody else wants for me. I wanted that baby! I. . . had already loved it."

There was a brittle silence. He didn't expect her to say anything like that. Who was this stranger that was spitting out words that he didn't want to hear? Where was the old Merriam? It was as if this new skinny person had it all mapped out and without his input. Suddenly he grew suspicious and realized that Merriam could already have a new fellow in her life.

"So, what's really been up, Ms. Slim?"

"My beautiful little fourth graders. I'm teaching summer school. And I've been dating a little too. Nothing serious right now. He's a new teacher at my school."

'I knew it,' he thought. He took a deep breath and followed with, "if it's nothing serious then why'd you tell me?"

"I thought I should tell you just in case you see his car in my driveway some evenings. Then you'll know not to stop in."

"His car? Merriam, how could you jump for joy and want to come to New Orleans to see me one minute and then tell me you've been dating the next?"

"Because it's nothing serious, yet. I'm just exercising my freedom a little like you do. At least I'm honest enough to tell you. That's probably a lot more than what you would do if you were dating someone else. Plus I've twiddled my thumbs long enough, Anwar. But I bet you haven't twiddled yours. You've probably been with a woman."

"That's not true!" Anwar's denial sounded like a bad actor's monologue.

"So phony. I know you had somebody. I could sense when you were with her. Oh yeah, you had somebody. I had a strange feeling come over me when I would call you."

"Oh really? Well I haven't been with anyone."

"You haven't had one woman since we've been apart? You're lying. I can see it in your eyes, Anwar. What do you take me for?"

He didn't respond. He simply turned away from her convicting eyes.

"I guess it's true what people say about you musicians. You all don't know how to settle down. You want your freedom much more than you want a wife and it doesn't take an Imhotep to figure that out. Last year has shown me a lot just by the way you jumped up and left from here. And before we try to build something again we just need to get real honest. We've lost something. I didn't even have the desire to kiss you. I can't explain that one."

Merriam was killing him with her honesty. He didn't want his body to desire her so badly; not if she didn't want him. She had new things that caught her attention. A man. Someone unlike him. A man that was fine with a simple life. Someone that wanted a boy to take to the barber. Wait! Merriam's nipples had stiffened and made an imprint through her gown. Was that arousal? Would she make a move? Huh! Neither would he. Damn. She'd been dating!

"Well, I'm going home. I'll see you in the morning."

Merriam left him sitting at the table heavyhearted, no differently than how he'd left her sitting when he went to New Orleans. 'But what the hell was she up to?' The coffee cup made a dull tap on an object as he sat it down. Merriam had left his door key on the table. She simply was not into him anymore. He felt like crying. It would be okay for him to date other women, even make love to them but his ego was too large to ever fathom Merriam dating or making love to another man. Maybe he did still love her deeply. And yet, he had been ready to throw away what he and she had had for Stanza, a woman he knew so little about. But that night Merriam appeared new and mysteriously attractive and the rejection was torturing him. He leaned further back in his chair and thought about the situation. *"Crunch!"* One leg of the chair broke in two and he fell to the floor. "Ouch! Shit!" Merriam had been right again! Good old Merriam! "Oh Merriam!" What had he been thinking? He trembled to think of them parting forever. 'Oh no.' He decided that he wasn't going to let her go that easily. Yes, he enjoyed his bachelorhood, yes he had had an exciting woman for a few weeks but he wasn't a fool. Merriam was a little bossy sometimes but he couldn't have found a more devoted woman than she. He would fight to win her back if he had to. Yes! He pounded his fist into his palm and imagined it to be the face of the new fellow she'd been dating. He downed the last bit of his coffee, rushed out and caught her door just as she was closing it. He turned off the kitchen light and carried her to bed.

Somebody called her house around 5:30a.m. Anwar picked up the receiver but did not speak.

"Hi, baby. You must be pretty sleepy. You always say hello," the baritone voice teased.

"Who is this?" Anwar demanded. The man simply said, 'wrong number' and hung up quickly.

"Who was it, sweetie?" Merriam asked groggily.

"It was your Ex. I want you to put that in check. Today! Merriam, are you listening?"

She smiled and cooed and was actually glad to see him react so strongly to the competition.

"I don't know. . . , I'll do what I can. It's not going to be all that easy; I mean, he's madly in love with me."

"Merriam, have you been to bed with him?"

"I could have. I could have gone to bed with anyone."

"Com' on now. Did you or did you not sleep with him?"

"Did you sleep with anyone in New Orleans?"

"No, dammit!" Anwar shouted.

"Well if you didn't, I didn't. If you did, I did. It all depends on you." She laughed hysterically.

"I'm not laughing. I didn't go to New Orleans to sleep around. I went there to work. I told you that."

"Anwar you are a liar!"

"Call me what you want but I don't want him calling anymore or—

"Wait one minute! Wait one damn minute! Are we married? And last I remembered that phone bill came in my name so I talk to whomever I want and you'd better understand that. I have been with you through thick and thin but you haven't been with me."

"You want this relationship to work or not, Merriam?"

"We had a relationship. What we have now is just lust. I need a man of the marrying kind but you want to act like a baby boy when I want to have a baby boy. A real baby boy. One that wears diapers and doesn't shave."

She turned her back on him. He rose and sat on the edge of the bed and lit a cigarette. He thought long and hard. Yes, he still loved Merriam but damn, did he want to marry her? Or anyone? After thinking for about fifteen minutes, he gathered his scattered clothing, found his shoes and went home. She sat up and smiled to no end. "Yeah, keepin' you on your toes, motherfucker," she spoke into the air. She giggled, plumped her pillow and went back to sleep.

The last time Anwar had tossed and turned in bed was when Bassetta was stolen. But Merriam's new male friend was on his mind and he imagined her standing under an altar in a wedding gown. He imagined her pregnant, and finally, he imagined her holding a baby boy, what she had wanted most. He felt pressed to do something. But what? Their relationship was over four years old and Merriam often complained about being the only woman around with a barren womb. She would say quite often, "next year, next year with or without you, Anwar, I am going to have a child. Why should I have to suppress the joys of motherhood because you don't want marriage? I'm going to find someone who does." But she never did.

Once she'd stopped taking her birth control pills. When she told Anwar she was two months pregnant he hit the ceiling and accused her of trying to ruin his career.

"I just want a child!" she screamed. "What's so wrong with having a baby?"

"And what's wrong with being a Mingus?" he shouted back. "I want to put my music on the map and be famous. I don't have time for a wife and babies. I'm not gonna deal with this. I won't Merriam! You have to do something!"

So a baby never happened. They never discussed where the little bulging belly went, how it became so flat again. The longing for a child never left her though. She began keeping her infant nephew, a lot. It was as though he was the replacement for the child she had wanted so badly. Anwar knew he had hurt Merriam and most women would have called him a 'low life' and would have broken it off with him—but now she knew a man that didn't mind marrying her and having babies. Maybe he should just let her go to the new fella, he rationalized. Maybe he didn't even deserve her anymore. The relationship was becoming more and more discordant anyway. Maybe he should try to get someone like Stanza. He had always desired a woman that was challenging and exciting and could sing and tour the world with him but he had had that in Stanza and there were so many problems that came with that package. And one thing for sure, he did love Merriam and would be a fool, big time, to just let some other man have her.

Merriam fixed breakfast at his house but he hadn't felt like talking to her. He kept thinking of the voice on the other end of the line and wondered if she had slept with the man. She would never tell him if she had. That's how she was. But then again, he would never tell her about Stanza. Still, it hadn't seemed right somehow that he didn't know about Merriam's love life. He was a man! He felt like he should know. Call him a 'double standards kind of guy if you wanted and he wouldn't give a damn. Suddenly a chilling thought came to him. What if Merriam were already carrying the man's child? He shuddered to think that it could happen. But the possibility was there if they had been sleeping together. He ate quietly, staring across the table at Merriam. She looked suspicious and squirmed and smiled as though she had a secret. She had a cell phone too. 'What did she need a cell phone for?' he wondered. He didn't even have a cell phone. And there she sat as if she was waiting on a call from somebody important and it surely wasn't him because he didn't even have the number. 'But maybe she was teasing him. Maybe the man was just a friend. Women often find ways to provoke jealousies in men. But he called her *baby*.' He finally rose from the table, took her hand and led her to the cylinders and phonograph. She was speechless.

Finally she said, "Sweetie, I can't believe this. How did you swing it? Never mind, tell me later. I have to get dressed."

But he wouldn't allow her to leave. He gently laid her on the bed and began making love to her again and didn't care if she would conceive. He was going to make sure the new teacher wouldn't get any signals from her. He had to make one thing perfectly clear to the man: that she belonged to him and not them.

Chapter 17
Bull's Crap

Chuckles and yelps were dulled by the sound of running water and a heavy shower curtain. 'Oh, the expression on Giles' face when he sees the cylinders!' He would first present him with the research on the marching bands, then Buddy's photos, the letters and last but not least, the wax cylinders and phonograph. He would play the cylinders for Giles then take everything to Beard and they would celebrate. For that occasion, he had brought Bassetta along. Afterwards he would store the items in the display case of the school's music department until plans to record and distribute Buddy's music had been made—and finally, he would return the items back to Buddy's home.

Giles had just downed a plate of chicken chow mein when Anwar entered. He took a sip of milk and while still chewing, he said, "Hey, Mr. Rasual, welcome back. I know ya got something good for me. Sit down. **Sit down**." Anwar smiled confidently.

"You always eat so sloppy, man?"

"Oh, am I messy? I can fix that."

Giles grabbed a moistened tissue and wiped his face until it turned red. There were spots of brown sauce he had missed but Anwar didn't bother to tell him. Giles gazed into Anwar's face tilting his head one way then another. He knew something was different. He held up his index finger but couldn't pinpoint anything and Anwar wasn't volunteering to talk about it. Then Giles noticed the two bulky items covered in muslin and mounted onto a hand truck.

"What the hell ya got there?"

"The surprise of your life, that's what."

"Oh yeah? We'll see. Alright, talk to me. How'd it go? Get any work done or all play?"

"I worked my ass off."

"Sure you did, sure. Prove it. Where's my research?"

Anwar held up a neatly bound book entitled, 'Jazzy Street Beats.'

"Ha! Your picture's gonna go right on the second page of the book with your name and endorsement. Yep. You deserve it. Let's have a look."

The phone rang at the same time Giles reached for the book. The caller was hysterical. It was a female professor and she was screaming in Giles' ear. He tried to calm her down but couldn't.

"Listen, hold on. I'm coming to your office. Just settle down. Be right back, Anwar. Don't move," Giles said nervously and he ran out completely unaware Buddy's cylinders were on that campus. Every jazz researcher would be filled with envy.

Anwar grew impatient waiting for Giles who had not returned for over ten minutes. Rising without true purpose, he made his way to the bookcase. There again set the research Giles had collected. It had been dated 1994. He would be able to update it, finally. Directly above his head was a blue and silver book bearing the title, 'Jazz', authored by Giles. It had been published in 1996. Anwar lifted it from the shelf and sat down to browse through it. There were many excellent pictures of early jazz artists. He gazed at the title of the third chapter and was immediately shaken. It read *'Jazz Is Not African American Music.'*

That title hit Anwar so hard that his whole head began to ache. 'If it ain't African American then what the hell is it?'

"It's African, that's what it is," he spoke aloud. "It's African music taken across the waters."

The book stated that '*a strange style of music evolved as a result of black people trying to play American music that they had never truly learned. It was invented by trial and error.*

"Oh Boy!" Anwar said, rolling his eyes toward the ceiling. "It was developed in Africa!"

As he made his way through the first few pages, he saw that it stated that '*black people meant to play European classical music but it was way over their heads. They didn't understand order, just chaos. The results were an accidental music that was played viciously without direction.*' It also stated, '*African Americans had popularized that sound only because they had no idea what real music was. Inadvertently, they took bits and pieces of classical music and kept filling them in with wrong notes*'.

'Wrong notes? It was improvisation. They were new notes. That's like paint on a canvass. It's a whole new picture than what's been given to you. It's always been an African thing to improvise and to be creative. It was an exciting way of presenting something back with the musician's feelings inside.' Anwar was getting jittery. 'Oh, Giles is up to something,' he thought. 'And why had the best readers both black and white turned to jazz soon after Buddy had introduced it if it didn't have direction? Cause it was amazing music, that's why. This book is crap! What else did Giles write'?

'*Improvised music,*' the book explained, '*originally had order. It had been rehearsed music, never spontaneous.*'

'Fuckin' lies! Improvisation does not have to be rehearsed! Giles has research on his desk to smash those lies, so why's he telling them?' The book continued, stating '*. . . when done so, it is not to be considered true music. Anything that is not written down is chaotic unless memorized perfectly.*'

'What? So now jazz has to be memorized'?

The book also stated that '*. . . improvisation was like*

forgetting the words and melody and making them up as one went along whether they had made sense or not. The results were clashing flats and sharps and weird tones and scales but 'certain' people had tried to validate the sound as a genre anyway. Bebop had been a classic example of that.'

Never had Anwar read such trash about jazz, such disgusting lies. 'Jazz is organized, technical and improvisation, period. Yes, it has complicated chord patterns and changes and timing. Some researchers had been vague, but not flat out liars. Why was Giles doing this? And what did he mean by certain people?' Anwar's head throbbed harder. 'Certain people? Black people!' He searched inside his pockets hoping that he had stuffed his cigarettes in one but they had been left in the car. He did find a peppermint and popped it into his mouth hoping the sugar would ease the pain that had crawled to the back of his neck. He read on.

'Black people became full blooded citizens, which meant they were to forget about things that came out of Africa.

'Full blooded? Oh really! And if so would that mean we should not even claim our African heritage? We're not immigrants. We didn't ask to come here and we didn't give up our culture willingly. And we kept a lot of it alive behind closed doors. But Giles, is saying that it's fine for American whites to claim their music but not fine for black people to claim theirs. Why won't he call European classical music American Music? Because it's not and neither is jazz. It came from Africa with black people! This book is menacingly evil. And so is Giles!'

That led Anwar to think about the lie claiming Christopher Columbus had discovered America when there were already people in America. Practically every history book claimed that and practically everybody believed that. 'So what were the indigenous people? Invisible?'

'All music has roots and jazz existed in Africa even before there was an America. And hadn't Giles understood that blacks had found ways during slavery to pass along their musical traditions? It was never accidental and vicious music. And it had always been blacks desire to play it openly once more and not just in fields where they labored or in secret. Surely Giles knew that. He just wasn't saying.' Fortunately, there were white jazz researchers who did write the truth and their works had made Anwar feel somewhat better. 'But Giles? He was a seething snake! It was just like Merriam had said: *Giles was a 'culture vulture.'*

"Why has it been so important for other's to discredit blacks of their contributions?" he mumbled. 'And somebody was always trying to take African roots out of African/African-American music. Our blues, rock, doo wop, soul, R & B, gospel, rap, jazz, and all other black rooted musical genres. That is crazy. Giles is in that group. He knows good and damn well jazz originated with black people, which was why wherever African people were taken throughout the diaspora, there appeared a form of jazz. We don't mind sharing our culture, but we do mind when people want to steal it and claim it as their own. We got a big problem with that! Jazz is black African music. It came with us! Point blank! Fuck Giles!'

Disgust and anger almost talked him into turning over Giles' heavy desk and tossing his work out of the very window Giles revered so much. 'Why can't people just be fair and give credit where credit is due? Could hatred and jealousy really run that deep?' He shuddered to think that every jazz book would state what Giles had written and the lie could actually grow as big as the lie about Christopher Columbus discovering America.

As he read on, he noticed that there was no mention of Buddy Bolden except to say *'he was never proven to be a real live person,'* which was bull.

Giles' motives had been woven in a masterful covert plan. Here he was sitting on mounds and mounds of factual research that he'd collected before that book had even been written. Yet, he had intentionally fabricated and modified that book to fit his own design. What Giles had recorded after discrediting this black person and that black person in his book was that *'the earliest jazz musicians were not black and that jazz is just a genre untalented musicians like to hide behind.'*

The cover flew off the book as it hit the wall with great impact. 'Destroy this damn thing,' he thought. He picked it up and threw it against the wall again. The girl with the green dreadlocks and his students had tried to warn him but he closed his ears. And no wonder Giles wanted him to do the research and endorse the book. With a black jazz professor's name and picture included, the book would appear more credible. 'Shit! Giles was going to use me!'

To think that he had been prepared to store Buddy's cylinders and phonograph in the school's display case for a little while made him cringe. Was he crazy? Would they have disappeared if he had? Ruth and Gifford had trusted him when they gave him Buddy's relics. They loved Buddy and understood his pulse, his passion and insatiability, and they saw that also in Anwar. 'No! Giles couldn't have that new research to twist and fabricate into lies. Not what he had gathered! Cultures will always be shared, of course, but when they are outright stolen, that is cause for much alarm. It was very clear to Anwar that Giles had much more in mind than writing a textbook. He planned to rewrite the history of jazz. Damn Giles!'

What textbook would Anwar put Buddy into? He thought intensely about that. Then the poem, 'Note On Commercial Theatre,' by Langston Hughes, came to mind. He remembered a line stating, 'someday somebody is going to write and talk about me'. Then it followed up with something like, 'I think that somebody will be me.' At that moment, Anwar made the decision to write a jazz textbook.

He would use authenticated facts.

He picked Giles' book off the floor, set it on the desk and jotted out a note stating, "I read excerpts from your book. I have vacated this position because you left me no choice." He mounted his items and left.

He knew he could be facing a lawsuit but then again, so could Giles because he had falsified Anwar's records as to grant him sabbatical leave while other professor's sabbatical requests had been denied. 'Rank abuse,' had been painted all over' Giles' position. He had actually hired Anwar for his own personal agenda. Let his authorities find out he had made him an Associate Professor minus experience, Giles and the University Provost might find themselves wearing stripes.

"Now what?" he wondered, as he cruised down the highway? He needed someone to talk to. Beard, of course! It had to be Beard. That's who he should have seen first anyway. Of course, he should have! He pulled over to a pay phone.

"Beard, it's Anwar, man. Yeah, I made it back home. I'm headed over to your place. I have something I know you'll be glad to see."

"Something like what?" Beard asked excitedly.

"It relates to jazz. That's all I can tell you right now. I should be there in a little while."

He had love letters, photos, two cylinders and a phonograph. And to think he was going to play Buddy's music for Giles before Beard had heard it. Nobody should have come before Beard. 'Beard introduced me to Buddy,' he reminded himself. 'I've got to be about the biggest fool in the world.' Suddenly, he felt very ashamed of himself. The vision he had began to make more sense than ever. It had told him that he had been out of his *black state of mind*.

Chapter 18
Buddy And His Chil'ren

Beard's place was cluttered with papers and books as usual. It smelled of greens and spicy meat and that meant dinner was on! He was an excellent cook, like Merriam, and Anwar had enjoyed many meals with him as they discussed jazz, especially after returning from a concert together. He'd often imagined Beard and Merriam having a cook-off while he was the sampler. He would test all the dishes and intentionally rule himself indecisive which would call for a rematch and he could be the sampler all over again.

Anwar rang the bell over and over. "Alright, alright. Lay off," Beard said, opening the door slowly.

"Got something for you, slowpoke," Anwar said, pushing his way through and walking inside regally. Beard followed anxiously and watched carefully as Anwar opened a case and unraveled the fabric around a cylinder. He presented the cylinder to Beard. Beard closed his eyelids tightly, clutched his heart, then sighed, "Buddy."

Anwar nodded, 'yes.'

Beard's tears flowed, Anwar's too. They hugged one another, like father and son, crying so fervently that one might have thought they were attending a funeral.

Beard watched unbelievably as Anwar placed the phonograph upon the table. When he pulled the letters and photographs out, Beard stumbled to the sofa and inhaled and exhaled deeply through his mouth.

"Alright now, heart attacks are not welcome, Beard," Anwar teased. He just looked up at Anwar so innocently, like a little boy that needed to be cared for. He had grown frail since his days of teaching. His children still lived out of town and although they came and took him home with them often, he had practically become a hermit after the death of his wife. Plus, very few of his students had gone back to see him or thank him for what he had given them. That disturbed Anwar. He thought maybe he and Merriam could sort of adopt him, just look out for him all the time. *That was if he and Merriam could patch things up.*

Both men appeared afraid to listen to the cylinder. Afraid that perhaps something could be shattered inside of them, something they'd held onto for years. Had Buddy been forced to play another genre? Could it have not been a true jazz style as some researchers had maliciously written? Had it been an uncategorized link between ragtime and jazz? No. Those researchers had to be biased. There was no way a man rooted in so much black culture, passion and creativity would allow anything other than jazz to represent him in a recording.

They both breathed hard for a few seconds and then Anwar attached the cylinder to the phonograph and started it up. It worked! It worked! They both froze. Buddy's horn was heard. It appeared that two more musicians played along with him, a guitarist and a bassist.

They barely breathed for the entire duration of the song. The recording was scratchy and inaudible in spots but they could hear Buddy's cornet clearly enough to know that it was the style that they loved. Jazz!

Beard shouted, "Go on, Buddy! That's right, play it brother!"

Anwar squalled, "bro' is playing his ass off, ain't he? Oh, sorry Beard. Play that Chas, Buddy! Play that Chas."

"Hey, Beard, I'll be right back!"

Anwar ran out to his car, got Bassetta and rushed back

in. "These cylinders can't be played too much but I say nobody deserves to hear it again like you and me. Take the bench, Beard. Let's jam with the King."

Beard hurried to his piano and he and Anwar played along with the recording, both feeling most privileged and honored to accompany the likes of Buddy. Beard's fingers swept up and down the keyboard as they had never done before while Anwar's fingers plucked and plucked Bassetta with his head bobbing so wildly that one would have thought he was being played by his instrument instead of the other way around. Finally their ultimate jam session came to an end.

"What are you going to do with all these things, Son?"

"Well, I'll record the cylinders and put copies in jazz archives around the world. I'm gonna start a fund. Every dime that this music makes goes back to the black side of New Orleans to help build it up. The cylinders and all the other stuff goes back too. I'm sure Buddy would want it that way. Maybe I could start a jazz museum with a few jazz musicians there and call it 'The New Orleans Museum of Jazz and African Rooted Music' or something like that."

"You could make it simple and just call it Music With African Roots," Beard responded.

"Yeah, that fits. It fits really well, Beard. Thanks, man."

"That's a wonderful thing that you're taking Buddy's music back to his home. I thought you were gonna sell it to some famous museum and make a lot of money."

"A year ago I would have done just that. But I've learned, Beard. Buddy is ours, man! Your Buddy and he's definitely 'my Buddy.' He belongs to our people. Unequivocally! We can share him but that's about it. His journey was about his black people! I had to learn that the hard way, Beard. And just think, he called *us*! Remember that day we cried over him? He was calling out to us then!"

"Yes, and now we have jammed with him. Amazing."

"It sure is," Anwar asserted, proudly. "His chil'ren."

"I always said you were the best student I ever had."

"You're darn right, I was. And your best student is going to write a jazz textbook too. We have to write the truth because there are a lot of people ready to write the lies. If we allow other people to write our history from their perspective they'll leave us out of it. Our people need to know how things really went down."

Anwar wrapped the items and the cylinders went back into their boxes. "Oh Beard, by the way, I visited Marie Laveau's tomb."

"Ah hah! And now you have Buddy's cylinders."

"Beard, do you believe—

"What do you mean, do I believe? Hell naw! But we did just jam with 'The King. I just think it was all meant to be."

"Yeah, me too. But the people, Beard. They believe in her. Really."

"Yeah, I know. But maybe they know something don't know."

"But I almost lost all this stuff, Beard. Remind me to tell you all about it one day. You won't believe the crap I went through to get it. You know it didn't come easy."

"Did you think that it would? Writing that book won't be so easy either but you have to write it. I wish I had wrote a textbook. I've always wanted to but teaching and taking care of my family just sort of absorbed me."

Anwar thought about how dedicated Beard was when he was a professor and how he had gone home and taken care of a sick wife for years. In spite of all his hardships, he pushed through and inspired in his students a passion that would last them a lifetime.

"Beard, you will write this book with me. You gave me this passion for jazz. Matter of fact, your name is going in as coauthor. And you're going to New Orleans with me too."

"I'd love that and you know I have a lot of research."

"Then get it off the shelves. Let's do this. But before we actually start writing, I'm gonna tie the knot with Merriam if she still wants me. I've broken her heart so many times that I feel ashamed of myself. And she's a good woman, Beard. It's time we start a family before we're too old."

"Well that's a good thing. So now when you get my age you'll have someone to call you, 'grandpa.' Now you don't want to compromise your dreams so be sure you're marrying the right woman. You got a great future ahead of you with the textbook and the museum. Emotions are some funny things, son. You're sure at the beginning and the next thing you know, love has gone out the window. Billie would say, *'it's don'turned off and gone.'*

"Yeah, she sure would. Billie always kept it real."

"You love Merriam?"

"I didn't think I did anymore but I was confused." He began telling him about Stanza.

"She was like a dream that I just couldn't seem to touch. I can touch Merriam and I know she can touch me. She keeps things real like Billie and I feel like I would have a pretty good life with her by my side. I would have been walking on eggshells with Stanza."

"You know this for sure? Be sure now. Saying 'I Do' is easy. Living 'I Do' is the hard part. I was married for over forty years to a fine woman and let me tell you, it was hard. Just be sure you're not supposed to be somebody else's husband. You have to ask yourself that question."

'Why did Beard have to say that?' Anwar's thoughts began racing. His father had always stressed the importance of marrying the right woman too but how could anyone know if they had the right mate until after they were married? People change. One thing for sure though, Merriam had been basically the same person from day one. He was the reason she had been making plans that didn't include him. He'd been selfish. He hadn't considered her feelings for a long time. But he would make it up to her and be a hell of a good husband. And father. 'As a wife,' he thought, Merriam would be supportive of his dreams as long as she felt loved. And if she treated their children half as good as she did her nephew and fourth graders, he'd have no worries about their emotional needs being met. With Stanza, hah! She'd have a problem dealing with her own emotional needs less lone a child's.'

"Beard, I won't be able to live that lie about having been faithful and look into Merriam's beautiful eyes. I love her too much to mislead her like that. And even if she has been with another man I would have to forgive her because I'm the one that pushed her into someone else's arms with my wishy-washy shit. I'm going to tell her tonight about Stanza and get it off my chest then let the cards fall where they may. Hopefully, they will fall in my direction. If she chooses to walk, then I will wish her well. It'll hurt me to my heart to let her go but I acted like an asshole."

"Women are forgiving, Son. The first time. But not the second time," Beard chuckled.

"It won't be a second time. And Stanza, Beard? She wasn't just any woman," Anwar said softly, adding a sigh, "she was a jazz vocalist. I didn't tell you that."

"Good God. I know she had you going."

"Morning, noon and night. When she sang I was in another world. She broke my heart though. She was so beautiful."

"If she hadn't broken your heart would you still want her?"

"No. She was just a fantasy, that's all. She was a one-hundred and fifteen pound enigma scatting incognitos over my head. When the music would end, she'd be gone."

"You're getting sensitive and writing poetry now?" Beard teased.

"I've always been a poet."

"You could have fooled me. In fact, you did fool me."

"I'm just being truthful, man. Wait a minute. Did I really say enigma and incognito? I can't remember ever using those words," Anwar laughed.

"Well, you did. I still hear pretty good for an old man.'

"Well anyway, Merriam is the woman for me. I don't have to guess about it anymore."

"Well on that note, I'm leaving it alone. By the way, who punched you in your jaw?"

"You noticed?"

"I noticed when you first came inside. I just didn't mention it."

"Well, we'll have to talk but I didn't get in a fight over a woman if that's what you think."

"Who said anything about a fight over a woman? You could have gotten into a bar brawl as far as I know. You just told on yourself." Beard laughed at Anwar.

"It wasn't over a woman. And I'm getting it fixed."

"Good, you need it fixed," Beard said playfully then moved slowly toward a small door. He disappeared into the pantry, fumbled on the shelf and reappeared with a bottle.

"Moonshine," he whispered, with a devilish grin.

"Moonshine? Really? Beard, since when'd you start drinking moonshine? Where'd you get that stuff anyway?"

"None of your business. But I've always kept a bottle for those rare and special occasions."

"Buddy drank moonshine. Did you know?"

"You think I didn't? Course he drank moonshine," Beard said, with another devilish grin. "Nothing sets the mood to jazz like the real McCoy."

Anwar lifted the bottle and held it to the beam of sunlight pouring through the window.

"Ain't nothing wrong with that bottle."

"I'm just checking it out. So this is moonshine?"

"You mean you haven't had moonshine before? Now just what kind of jazz musician are you that never drank moonshine? You're too pitiful boy."

Anwar laughed and bowed then opened the cupboard, looked around on the crowded shelves and caught two wine glasses by their stems.

"What? Wine glasses?" Beard groaned. "No. You don't drink moonshine outta wine glasses. Buddy could tell you that much."

Beard lifted two heavy jars from the cupboard.

"You drink moonshine out of jelly jars. It's a backwoods kind of thing. Keep tradition going, boy."

"Jelly jars? You're kidding. How old are these things Beard?"

"Don't know for sure. My grandmother had them before I was born. Pour the sauce, son."

Anwar poured the glistening liquid. He smelled it and took a little sip and frowned. Beard snickered. They made their way to the back porch. Beard sat on the small glider while Anwar sat on the porch floor and stretched his long legs across the stairs. They did not speak. Words would serve no purpose. The two men simply stared at the blue sky as it slowly descended into twilight. Buddy Bolden's cornet still rang in their heads, 'calling his chil'ren home.' Their passion had been peaked. They would breathe evenly whenever they spoke of Buddy. Jubilantly. The world would finally hear his song.

They closed their eyes and sipped slowly from the lopsided jelly jars.

THE END

By Ife-Gail F. Young

References

The Jazz Life Of Dr. Billy Taylor; Dr. Billy Taylor & Teresa Reid 2013 (Origins of Jazz See Chapter 1 - 'Beginnings' - pgs. 1-2)

In Search Of Buddy Bolden, Marquis; Donald, 1978

Buddy Bolden & The Last Days of Storyville; Barker, Danny 2001

Music Is My Mistress; Edward Kennedy Ellington (Duke) 1973

Princess Noire-The Tumultuous Reign of Nina Simone; by Nadine Cohadas, 2010

Other tidbits of factual material were drawn from historical documents, interviews, books, films and journals on Charles 'Buddy' Bolden

Thank you for purchasing this Natroy Publishing item. If you have enjoyed this book, we would appreciate you recommending it to others, schools, libraries and bookstores. There will be many more titles to choose from, as our entire collection is scheduled for release. We publish children's, teens and adults literature. We also publish theatrical plays, poetry, and CD's.

Please visit our website: www.natroypublishing.com for more information about our literary collection.

NATROY PUBLISHING

We offer exciting, book signings that include storytelling, music, songs, workshops and skits. Consider scheduling a book signing for the author at your site and give your patrons something a little special.

For further information, please contact us at natroypub@gmail.com

Always thinking about the next project...

Ife-Gail F. Young, an award winning writer, was born, raised and educated in Cleveland, Ohio. She has many titles and credits to her name, including stories, plays, poetry, skits, novellas, novels, essays and songs. We find no need to give her unending praises and accolades as her numerous refreshing works have spoken for themselves. They are superb thought-provoking, bold and refreshing writings for children, teens and adults. Her literature has the power to enchant the reader with its unique plots and characters that are woven into a magical imagery with an unpretentious and fluid style.

Her plays have appeared on stages in several states, including New York. In addition, Ife is also an actress, vocalist, storyteller, illustrator, and a 'lightweight guitarist.' She holds a B.A. in Dramatic Arts and is set upon completing a joint Master's & Ph.D. Program in Literature. She awaits the release of a movie she scripted in 2012-2013.

She currently resides in NYC

198

YOU CAN PURCHASE
'MY BUDDY'
And Other Works By *Ife-Gail F. Young* At:
www.amazon.com

Search For: Gail Young
Or Book Title.

OTHER WORKS
"Journey Through A Zigzagged Forest In A Dark Faced ~~Woman~~ Girl" Vol. 1-- A collection of 2 unusual stories drawn from the black experience, addressing political and social concerns.

"Journey Through A Zigzagged Forest In A Dark Faced ~~Woman~~ Girl" Vol. 2-- A collection of 2 bizarre stories drawn from the black experience. They address political and social concerns as well as shed light on institutions such as marriage and religion.

"Journey Through A Zigzagged Forest In A Dark Faced ~~Woman~~ Girl" is an ongoing adults short-story series. New Vols. are added regularly. EXCELLENT REVIEWS!!! All stories are written by Ife-Gail F. Young

"Bina and the Beanpole Vols. 1,2,3" –A coming of age children's chapter book series with illustrations that empowers, inspires, promotes, history, unity, literacy and healthy values while helping to steer children (specifically, African American youth) toward greatness. Vols. 1, 2, & 3... A MUST HAVE FOR AFRICAN-AMERICAN YOUTH!

"After All Is Said And Done" – This novel extracts from the 'black experience' and takes the reader on a myriad of events. It discloses lies, challenges tradition, contains love, horror, street scenarios, solutions and triumph.. It is thought provoking, unique, seduces the emotions and captures the imagination. SOON TO COME

www.ingramcontent.com/pod-product-compliance
Lightning Source LLC
Chambersburg PA
CBHW031332170626
46807CB00002B/667